THE WINDS OF AUTUMN

THE WINDS OF AUTUMN

JANETTE OKE

THE WINDS OF AUTUMN
A Literary Express, Inc. Book
(a subsidiary of Doubleday Direct, Inc.)
Reprinted by special arrangement with:
Bethany House Publishers
A Ministry of Bethany Fellowship International

PRINTING HISTORY
A Bethany House Publication / March 1987
The Janette Oke Collection / 1997

If you would be interested in purchasing additional copies of this
book, or have any questions concerning the Janette Oke
Collection and your membership, or if you would like to
correspond with the author, please contact us at:

The Janette Oke Collection
Literary Express, Inc.
1540 Broadway
New York, NY 10036
Telephone #973-473-4800

ISBN: 1-58165-143-0

Printed in the United States of America

With love
to my Uncle Ralph Steeves,
just because
he's special.

JANETTE OKE was born in Champion, Alberta, during the depression years, to a Canadian prairie farmer and his wife. She is a graduate of Mountain View Bible College in Didsbury, Alberta, where she met her husband, Edward. They were married in May of 1957, and went on to pastor churches in Indiana as well as Calgary and Edmonton, Canada.

The Okes have three sons and one daughter and are enjoying the addition to the family of grandchildren. Edward and Janette have both been active in their local church, serving in various capacities as Sunday-school teachers and board members. They make their home in Didsbury, Alberta.

Table of Contents

Characters

Joshua Chadwick Jones—When Josh's parents were killed in an accident while he was still a baby, he was raised by his grandfather and his great uncle Charlie on the family farm. Though Aunt Lou was not many years older than Josh, being a latecomer to the Jones family, she also took delight in caring for young Josh, and he saw her as a friend and a mother rather than an aunt.

Lou Jones Crawford—Josh's aunt whom he had fought to keep with the family unit in *Once Upon a Summer*. Pretty and vivacious, yet with deep concern for others, Lou was a fitting helpmate for the young minister she married.

Grandpa—the grandfather of Joshua and father of Lou.

Uncle Charlie—the quiet yet supportive brother of Grandpa. He had never married but worked along with Grandpa on his farm.

Gramps—Josh's great-grandfather who had come west to live with his two sons, his granddaughter Lou and great-grandson Joshua after the death of his wife.

Nat Crawford—the young pastor Lou married. Josh now spends his weeks in town with Lou and Nat in order to continue his education in the town school.

Pixie—the answer to Josh's dream for a dog of his own. She was given to Josh by Gramps who went to great effort to find Josh a second puppy after his first pup was accidentally killed.

Chapter 1

An Autumn Surprise

I don't remember a prettier fall than the one we had the year I was fifteen. The long Indian summer days stretched on into October with only enough sprinkles of rain to keep the flowers blooming in Aunt Lou's flower beds and the lawn green enough to contrast with the yellows and golds of the autumn trees and bushes. Even the leaves seemed reluctant to "tuck in" for the winter and kept clinging to the branches week after week in all their fine, colorful array. The sun warmed up the air by noon each day, and the nights were just nippy enough to remind us that we'd best be spending our time getting ready for winter instead of loafing along beside the crik, pretending that this good weather would stay with us forever.

The farmers in the area took in all the crops, the women cleaned out their large farm gardens, we stayed loafing by the crik whenever we could, and still the good weather held. People started talking summer picnics and parties again, but I guess no one wanted to exert themselves enough to do the fixing, for the days went by and no one actually had a picnic—we all just sat around in the sun or took long, lazy walks through the colorful countryside.

As you probably have figured out by now, my favorite place was down by the crik. I took my fishing pole and headed there every chance I got. Most often Gramps, my great-grandfather, went along with me. He likes fishing—and loaf-ing—most as much as I do. The only thing that got in the way of my fishing trips was school. Most all the area boys my age had given up on school and gone off to farm with their pa's or to work in a store or something, but I still hung in there.

Part of it was due to my aunt Lou encouraging me a lot. She was sure I had a good head and kept telling me that it would be a waste, should I not use it. Her husband, my uncle Nat, chimed right in there with her. Since he was the parson in our little town church, I felt that if anyone knew the im-portance of education, my uncle Nat would be the man. He had gotten his the hard way, having to work his way through school and seminary on accounta he didn't have a ma or pa to see him through, them having died when he was still quite young.

Me, I had it easy. I not only had Lou and Nat but I had Grandpa, a great-uncle Charlie and my Gramps, my great-grandpa. All of them were right keen on me getting all the education I could.

It wasn't a problem to me. In fact, I really liked book learning, even if our school wasn't a very big one and most of the students were young kids or girls. Oh, a few of the boys still attended—like my best friend, Avery Garret. He didn't care too much for school and didn't know what he wanted to do with any schooling that he did get. I figured he just continued on because I was there—and, then, there was a certain amount of fun to be had at school. I mean, with all the girls still going and all.

Then there was Jack Berry. His pa was bound and deter-mined that Jack would be a doctor. Jack wasn't so sure. Truth was, he kinda had his heart set on being a sailor. Only there wasn't any water handy-like, any big water that is. So he didn't know just how he was going to manage to get on a boat—at least a boat any bigger than the rough-looking little two-oar one left down on the small pond near the town for anyone's use who might want to do some rowing.

Willie Corbin was still going to school, too. I wanta tell

you about that Willie. He was the biggest rascal in our community when he was younger. Used to get himself in all
kinds of trouble. Folks thought that he never would amount
to anything but most likely end up in some jail or something.
Me, I knew that Willie wasn't really bad; he just liked to
have fun, that was all. But that all changed when Willie
decided he'd rather spend his future in heaven than hell.

This happened way back after my uncle Nat preached his
first sermon in our church. He had just been asked to be our
new minister. Willie straightened himself right around and
never did go back to his wild ways. I figured if God could
make such a change in the likes of Willie Corbin, then He
ought to be able to handle almost anyone. Anyway, Willie
about had his mind made up that God wanted him to be a
missionary. Willie found studying rather hard, but one had
to admire him. He kept plugging away at it, determined to
prepare himself for some kind of work with heathen people
somewhere.

Those were the three fellows from my old country school
who were still hanging in there. Then there were four older
guys from town. We all hung around together, but I spent
most of the time with my old buddies, mostly I guess because
they were also from our small church. A couple of the town
fellas were a little "wild," according to Aunt Lou, and though
she didn't forbid me to see them or anything like that, still
she did prefer me to make close friends with the church
young folks.

I didn't complain. I liked the church kids and we had us
a lot of fun with our corn roasting, sleigh riding, skating on
the pond and such.

It seemed hard to believe that me and Pixie, my little dog,
had already been two years with Aunt Lou and Uncle Nat
in town. We didn't stay in town all the time. Whenever the
weather was good—and as I said, it was good most of the
time that fall—we went on out to the farm for the weekend
to spend time with Grandpa, Uncle Charlie and Gramps, who
batched together there.

I would have been hard put to try to say which place I

liked best. While I was in town during the week I counted the days till the weekend when I could get back out on the farm again and chop some wood, or go to the pasture for Bossie, the milk cow I had milked so many times myself. I even enjoyed the squealing and grunting of the pigs as I sloshed the slop into their troughs. The chickens seemed to sort of sing their clucking when I poured out their water and grain.

Then as soon as Sunday night came around, I found myself hardly able to wait to get back to town and Aunt Lou and Uncle Nat again. I wondered what Aunt Lou had fixed for Sunday dinner and if she'd saved a piece of pie or an apple dumpling for me. I wondered if Uncle Nat had been called out on some sick call and I hadn't been there to harness Dobbin for him. I thought of all kinds of things that I wanted to ask them or tell them when I got back. You'd think I'd been gone for days the way I chomped to get back again. The truth was, I had just seen both of them at the church service that very morning.

So that was the way I spent the fall, going back and forth, back and forth, and trying to grab the best of two worlds with both hands, so to speak. I would have tired myself plumb out if it hadn't been such a long, lazy-feeling kind of fall. Even after every lick of work was done, we still had us lots of good weather for catching up on just loafing around.

Only one thing wrong with that kind of weather. It sure made it hard to concentrate on studying. I had to take myself in hand every other day, it seemed, and just make myself sit down and study. And then another strange thing happened. Miss Williams, a maiden lady who had been teaching in our school for almost forever, went and threw in a surprise that nearly rocked the whole community. She was getting married, she said, just like that!

Now, no one in his right mind ever picked Miss Williams for the marrying kind. I mean, why would you? She had lived for years and years all alone and looked like she was enjoying it, and then, real sudden-like, she says she is getting married. To a sweetheart of some thirty-seven years, she says. Now, no one in the town knew anything at all about this fella. We'd never even heard of him. But that didn't stop Miss Williams any. She was quitting, she said, and she never gave notice or anything, just packed up her books and her bags and took the train back to some eastern city to marry this man.

Well, that left us without a teacher. There weren't none of us sitting around grieving much. Not even me who liked school. Jack Berry didn't try to hide his enthusiasm—he just whooped right out. A couple of the girls gave him a real cross look, but he didn't care. He whooped again and threw his plaid cap up into the air.

"Well," demanded Jack, "what we gonna do with this here unexpected blessing?"

"What do you mean?" asked Willie. He was already having enough trouble working his way through English without losing precious time. "Blessing? Not a blessing far as I'm concerned. Miss Williams was an okay teacher. Wisht she would have stayed around and finished the job."

I figured with Miss Williams already being there for thirty-seven years that she had probably stuck with the job about as long as anyone could expect her to. But even though I felt sorry for Willie, I couldn't hide my grin. It sure did seem like a blessing. I mean with the weather beckoning one outside all the time and all. Who knew when we might have winter set in and maybe then we wouldn't see the sun again for months? We could catch up on our studying then.

"Well," Jack asked again, "what do we do with this here— a—hardship?"

Even Willie had to smile at that, and the first thing we knew we were all laughing. When we finally settled down we busied ourselves with some serious planning.

"I s'pose I'll go on out to the farm," I said. "I always do on holidays or anything."

Jack lived just on the edge of town and there weren't as many things to keep a boy busy at his place, his folks having no livestock or crops or anything.

"Iffen I go home my pa'll want me to keep my nose in a book. Might as well be back in school," complained Jack.

"Fact is, I'd be better off in school. At least there we get recess."

Willie gave Jack a withering look. Jack had the brains if he just would use them, and I think it bothered Willie some that he had to work so hard for his average grade while Jack just fooled away his time and didn't even care what grade he got.

"Guess I'll have me plenty a good fishin' time," I continued, hoping to break the tension some.

"We could all get together for some football," put in Willie. He loved football and was good at it, too, in spite of the fact that none of us had any equipment to play the game and our folks were always worrying that someone might get hurt.

Avery spoke up then. "I've been thinkin' for a long time that it sure would be fun to backpack up along the crik and spend a night or two out campin'."

"Great idea," I practically hollered. I wondered why I hadn't thought of it long ago. It surprised me some to hear Avery mention it. He had never talked about it before. I had never been on an overnight hike, and with the woods looking like they did, it sounded like a first-rate idea.

Jack and Willie were about as excited as I was.

"Do you think our folks would let us?" asked Willie.

"Why not? We're already fifteen. 'Bout time we were allowed to do somethin' on our own."

I agreed. I suppose I would have been pressing to get the chance ages ago if I had just thought of it.

"Let's ask," said Jack. "They can't do no more'n say no."

The thought of them saying no just about made me feel sick inside now that the idea had begun to work on me. They just had to say yes! They *had* to!

"Who you gonna ask?" Avery was saying, and I suddenly realized he was speaking to me.

"Huh?" I grunted.

"You gonna ask your aunt Lou or your grandpa?"

I shrugged my shoulders. "I dunno. I'm at Aunt Lou's right now."

"Think she'll let you go?"

I thought about it. Aunt Lou was understanding enough—but she was a bit protective as well. Would she understand how much it meant to a boy to go off camping on his own? I switched my thoughts to my grandpa. He was a swell person, about as kind a fella as a boy could want to have watching over him. But I was sure he had never thought of taking off into the hills on a camping trip even if the fall work was all done. Seemed to me that he might favor me staying with the books as well.

"I dunno," I said again.

"Well, at least you've got a choice," said Avery. "Me, I've got to convince my ma. If I can sell her on the idea, she'll work it out with pa."

One thing I knew for sure, I didn't have a ma and pa to talk it over with.

"Look," said Jack Berry, "can you fellas come over to my house after your chores are done tonight? We gotta get our heads together and plan our attack."

Crazy Jack! He liked to make everything sound like we were all in a war against our folks or something, but nevertheless we all nodded our heads and agreed to try to get some time with one another over at Jack's house after we hauled the water and carried in the wood and coal.

We parted then. I think we were all sort of holding our breaths. I looked again toward the distant woods as I swung through the gate at Aunt Lou's. Boy, did they look inviting. I could visualize, from where I was, just where the crik cut through the hills and swung around to the south. I could almost hear the rustle of the gold and red leaves and feel the gentle breeze on the skin of my cheek.

A crow called, off in the distance somewhere, and I wondered why it hadn't already left for the South. Guess it just wanted to hang around and enjoy the good weather. Boy, the woods and fields really drew a body on such a day! I could hardly settle myself down to filling the woodbox and the coal scuttle.

Chapter 2

Pleading Our Case

I didn't say much to Aunt Lou while I wolfed down the cookies and milk she had out for me. She had already gotten the word that Miss Williams was done—had left just like that and our school was without a teacher in the middle of a term.

"It's a shame, that's what it is," remarked Aunt Lou. I guess she might have been repeating what everyone else on our block was saying, for she suddenly checked herself. She thought for a moment in silence and then continued in a lower voice, sort of confidential-like, "I think it's exciting that Miss Williams has finally made up her mind to marry the man who has been her friend for so many years. It must have taken courage. I do hope they will be happy together."

Aunt Lou's eyes wandered to the tintype of her own wedding on the mantel. I looked at it too, and even their proper-like expressions couldn't hide the light in her eyes or the triumph in Uncle Nat's. Her eyes now got a little misty, and then she sort of shook her head and spoke quietly. "It's just too bad it had to be in the middle of the school year like this, though."

Still, I knew Aunt Lou was quite ready to forgive Miss Williams for her small departure from accepted behavior for teachers.

She stood up.

"Well, it shouldn't be for too long," she said as though to comfort me. "The School Board has already called a meeting. They expect to have a new teacher here in no time." She reached out and patted my shoulder.

I tried to look properly sorrowful and downed the last of my milk.

"Better get at my chores," I said to explain why I was in such a hurry. "Some of us fellas plan to go to Jack's for a little while tonight. Sort of plan how we will handle this— this time off—without a teacher—an' all."

Lou smiled her approval. "Good for you!" she encouraged. "It's nice to see you boys are responsible enough to work it out. Even with school out for a while, I'm sure you won't suffer much with that kind of an attitude."

I nodded agreeably. I wasn't expecting to suffer much ei- ther—that is, if we could talk our folks into letting us do what we had in mind.

I hurried through my chores and opened the kitchen door wide enough to call to Aunt Lou that I was leaving but would be back in plenty of time for supper. She called back a cheer- ful response, the approving smile in her voice. I felt a little funny about it. I mean, here she was thinking we were plan- ning on how we could keep up with our studies, and we were thinking on how we could get as far away from our books as possible in the short time we had.

Swishing through the leaves on the ground, I didn't let it trouble me for too long. After all, I hadn't actually told Aunt Lou that we were thinking on *studying*. She had come up with that idea herself.

I was the first one to Jack's house. He was loafing out under the apple tree in his yard, a geometry book in his hand. I knew he had been sent out there to study. When I appeared he laid aside all pretense of looking at the book and motioned me over to join him.

"Well?" he demanded.

"Aw, I ain't said nothin' yet," I told him. "Have you? I mean, I thought we were gonna meet to plan things first an'—"

"Exactly!" said Jack.

"Aunt Lou thinks I'm comin' over here to plan how I'm gonna keep up in my schoolwork," I said rather sheepishly.

"Did you tell her that?" asked Jack, his eyes narrowing to little slits.

" 'Course not!" Made me a little mad at Jack. He knew very well I didn't lie none.

"Then you can't help how she figures it," shrugged Jack.

"Guess—not," I sort of stammered. "Still, I wish she hadn't seen it that way. Might make it harder when we do ask an' all."

Jack didn't look quite so cocky. "Sure hope not," he said, and I knew he saw my point.

This time I couldn't shake my uncomfortable feeling. I had never been untruthful with Aunt Lou, and I sure didn't want to start now, even if it did cost me the planned hike.

Avery joined us, puffing from his run and his breathless question turned my thoughts back to our planned trip. "Who's gonna be the cook?"

What in the world was he talking about?

"Who's gonna cook?" he asked again, his head swiveling between us. "We gotta have someone to cook or we don't go."

Jack was the one to respond. "We'll all cook."

Avery looked doubtful. "I can't cook," he stated flatly and then added skeptically, "An' I'll bet you can't either."

"Don't be crazy!" Jack scoffed. "It don't take a cook to fix a meal over'n open fire. You just stick it over the flame and that's it."

"You ever tried it?" asked Avery, persistent.

Jack gave him a dark look. "Thought you was the fella who was so all fired rarin' to go. Why you gettin' so worked up now? Stay home if you want," he said sarcastically, and Avery quickly changed his tack.

"Guess we could take along a loaf a bread and some cheese," he stated, but he didn't sound too enthusiastic.

"I'm plannin' to eat fish," I announced on a positive note.

Avery never had been fond of fish or fishing.

"Who'll cook 'em?" he asked me.

I was getting a little tired of Avery's gloomy persistence too.

"I'll cook 'em, that's who."

"You done it before?"

He had me there. My job was to catch them. It was Aunt Lou or Grandpa or Uncle Charlie who had done the cooking of them. I hadn't even cleaned a fish on my own. Well, I was game to give it a try. Anybody could clean and cook a fish.

Willie arrived just then and saved me the bother of convincing Avery.

The four of us settled down on the green lawn of the Berry backyard, our legs crossed in front of us Indian style. We proceeded to call to order, so to speak, our little meeting to make plans for the coming camp-out.

Since none of us had ever been on one before, we didn't know just how to approach the planning. Willie reached into his jeans pocket and came up with a stub of pencil and a sheet of folded paper. We all praised him some for his good thinking, and then we looked at one another. Jack sort of took charge.

"First of all we gotta figure what we're gonna need," he said, and that sounded sensible enough to the rest of us.

"Blankets," Jack started in, as though he had been doing more camp-out thinking than geometry studying while he was waiting for us to join him.

"Yeah," agreed Avery, "it gets pretty cold at night."

Willie scribbled "blankets" on one side of the paper.

"Food," went on Jack to Avery's energetic nod.

" 'Food' is too general. We gotta be 'pecific," said Willie, waiting with his pencil poised in the air.

None of us had ever done any meal planning before.

"Bread," ventured Avery.

Willie's pencil scratched again.

"Cheese," continued Avery.

"Bread and cheese! You crazy? I ain't living for days on bread and cheese," Jack contradicted.

"Well, you say what you want then!" snapped Avery. "Don't hear no bright ideas from you."

Willie interrupted before Jack and Avery had time to really get in a fuss. They never had been able to get along very well.

"I've got 'bread and cheese'; now what else do we want?"

"We'll need some butter 'n flour 'n salt 'n pepper for fryin' the fish," I put in rather knowledgeably. I had watched Aunt Lou mix the ingredients and put the floured fish in the sizzling butter many times, and her fried fish always tasted great.

"An' what iffen you don't catch any fish?" questioned Jack in a smart-aleck fashion.

"Then I guess you just eat bread and cheese," I threw back at him.

"We need pans for cooking—a fryin' pan and a kettle of some kind," cut in Willie to keep things from getting out of hand.

"Matches!" shouted Avery in a burst of inspiration.

We all gave him looks of appreciation. Matches at a campsite we would need all right.

Our list continued on to the back of the sheet, and before I knew it Mrs. Berry was calling Jack in for supper and the rest of us realized we'd better be getting home to our suppers, too.

Avery and I left Jack's yard on the run. Willie trotted off the other direction. It was hard to run and talk at the same time, so we didn't say a whole lot to each other.

"When you gonna ask?" Avery puffed.

"Dunno," I gasped out.

"Who you gonna ask?" went on Avery.

I shook my head. "Not sure yet," I admitted.

Truth was, I still wasn't clear on just which of my kin might make the best ally. I would sort of need to feel my way.

"Well, we can't wait," puffed Avery. "That ol' School Board is likely to go and rustle up a teacher 'fore we even get a chance to enjoy the break."

Avery was breathing hard after that long speech. I knew he was right, but I also disliked being pressured.

"I'll ask," I told him firmly; "don't you worry none about it."

We parted company at the end of Cottonwood Street, Avery heading off one direction and me the other. I looked at the sky as I ran on. I was afraid I was going to be late for supper, and though Aunt Lou might not scold, it sure wouldn't help my cause none.

I pulled into the lane that led past the parsonage and into the backyard just as Uncle Nat was dismounting Dobbin. I came to a halt beside him, struggling some to catch my breath.

"Whoa," said Nat. "Where you coming from in such a hurry?"

I waited a spell till I could talk a bit more evenly and then answered, "Been over at Jack's house—thought I might've stayed longer'n I intended. 'Fraid I was late for supper."

"Well, so am I," stated Nat, but he didn't seem worried none. "Mrs. Miranda took a bad turn again."

"Is she okay?" I asked.

"Seems to be fine again now."

I thought it must be at least once a week Uncle Nat was called to the Willises to say a prayer for "the departing Mrs. Miranda," as old Grandma Willis was called. She never had needed the final prayer yet, but then, I reckoned, someday she would and who could know just when that day might be?

I took up the reins hanging from Dobbin's bridle and waited for Uncle Nat to slip the saddle; then I led the horse toward the small barn and the stall that waited for him.

Even though Dobbin had gone about ten miles out to the Willis place and back, he still walked into the barn with a spring in his step. As always, I admired the horse. Gramps had bought him for Uncle Nat and Aunt Lou along with a sharp-looking little one-horse buggy. When Uncle Nat went alone, he usually rode the horse, though, instead of hitching up the rig. It was faster and he figured it saved the horse some too.

When we got to the barn I slipped Dobbin's bridle off and changed it for a halter. Uncle Nat reached for the currie comb and brush to give the horse a brisk rubdown. Without waiting to be asked, I crawled over the manger and forked in enough hay for the horse's supper. Then I measured out his chop. I had done this many times, so I knew just how much was needed.

"Hear you're without a teacher," commented Uncle Nat as the two of us worked side by side.

"Yeah," I responded without much emotion.

Nat smiled. "When I was your age I suppose I would've been rejoicing over having some free time—making all sorts of plans as to what I would do with it."

I didn't answer.

"This is really unusual for you," Uncle Nat went on reflectively. "No school at a time of year when there is no more farm work to be done. How do you plan to fill in those long, boring days?"

I knew he was funning me some, but I also saw it as a chance—a chance to maybe put in a word for the plans we had been making.

"Well," I said, real casual-like, "the fellas and me've been talkin'. Thought it might be a good time to try that there hike and—and camp-out we've been hopin' to work in."

I glanced from Dobbin, who was busy cleaning up his oats, to Uncle Nat. He never missed a stroke with the brush.

"Camping? Don't remember your mentioning camping."

"Well, no, we haven't," I hurried on. "Whenever the weather's been good enough, there was crops and garden still to be tended. But, just as you said, that work is all done this fall. And—and truth is," I finished in a rush, "I hadn't really thought on it before." I felt I needed to be totally honest with Uncle Nat.

Uncle Nat just nodded his head.

"We thought this might be a real good time," I pressed my point.

Then I checked myself. I didn't want to seem too eager—too pushy.

"Who's doing the planning?" asked Uncle Nat.

"Me n' Avery, n' Willie n' Jack," I blurted out.

Uncle Nat smiled a soft, teasing smile.

"When you give that list to your aunt Lou," he said, "I'd advise you to say, 'Avery, Willie, Jack and I.'"

I ducked my head. I'd been corrected on that particular grammatical error many times—especially by Aunt Lou.

"Where're you going?" asked Uncle Nat next.

My heart sort of skipped a bit. He had said, "Where're you going?" just like it had already been settled.

"Thought we'd follow the crik up into the hills where it starts at the spring," I answered, trying to make it sound like it had all been carefully figured out and approved. "Well, I just thought of it now," I continued in my efforts toward honesty, "but I think the fellas'll agree."

Uncle Nat nodded.

He turned then and put the currie comb and brush back up on the peg on the wall, gave Dobbin one more sound pat and nodded for me that we'd better get in to our supper.

I followed, just a bit hesitantly. I wasn't sure whether I'd won the round or not. Did Uncle Nat understand the need of a boy to get off on his own? Would he support me if it came to convincing the rest of the family?

We were almost to the house before he reached out a hand and let it rest on the top of my shoulder.

"Sounds like a great idea to me," he commented. "If I didn't have so many duties here at the church this week, I'd be right tempted to join you."

I let out my breath in a whoosh. Uncle Nat was on my side! That should count for something, at least. For the first time, I began to hope that I really might get to go.

Chapter 3

A Little Help

All the way out to the farm the next morning, Saturday, I felt my insides squirming a bit. I don't know why I was so nervous. I guess I wanted that camping trip far more than I supposed I would. I mean, I had never even thought of going camping until the day before when Avery suggested it, and now I was all het up about it. At the time I didn't even stop to wonder about Avery. He had never been one to care much for the out-of-doors that I was aware of. He didn't even like to fish, and yet here he throws out this surprise dream of his. But, as I said, I didn't think about that side of it till later.

I was busy thinking about me. More than anything in the world I wanted that camping trip. I don't know when I had ever wanted anything so much in my life except maybe when I had wanted a dog. Or when I had wanted to keep Aunt Lou instead of marrying her off to some local fella who wouldn't even fully appreciate what he was getting.

Well, I had my dog. Gramps had seen to that. I held Pixie closer to my chest and stroked the soft hair under her chin while she wiggled and strained against me. Even she, who loved to be cuddled, didn't like being held that close.

And as for Aunt Lou's marrying, when it came right down to it, I highly approved of the fella she had chosen. I felt pretty close to Uncle Nat myself. In fact, I dared to hope he might put in a word for me if it came down to arguing my case with the three menfolk at the farm.

We turned the horse and buggy down the lane, and my stomach did another turn as well. It wouldn't be long now until I would know one way or the other.

Grandpa met us at the front gate that opened up to the old farm home. He smiled his welcome from ear to ear and reached out to hug Aunt Lou. She had her arms full of baking like she always did when she visited the farm, but she accepted the hug anyway, giving Grandpa a kiss on his weathered cheek. Then Grandpa shook Nat's hand firmly and turned to me.

"So yer without a teacher, eh, Boy?" he said.

He still called me "boy" even though I felt I had outgrown that name. Still, I didn't resent it none the way Grandpa said it.

I just nodded my head.

"We heard the news," Grandpa said to Uncle Nat. "Was plannin' to come on in an' pick Josh up this mornin'. Hope it didn't mean a special trip for ya."

Uncle Nat just smiled. "Lou was anxious to come out and check on you anyway. I had some time this morning, and we plan to stop in at the Curtises on the way back to town and see that new baby."

We were met on the porch by Gramps, who patted my shoulder and hugged Aunt Lou. I could hear Uncle Charlie clattering dishes in the kitchen and guessed it was his turn for kitchen duties. He stepped to the door, dish towel in one hand and a pot in the other.

After our hellos Lou moved to set down her baking and put on the coffeepot. It didn't matter how long it was between visits, she still took over the kitchen whenever she stepped in the door.

We all settled into comfortable spots around the room.

"So what's this we hear about your school being closed, Joshua?" asked Gramps. Him being from the city and all, he was real interested in my education. The conversation turned to the school and the need for a teacher since Miss Williams up and left to marry her longtime sweetheart.

"Any idea how long it might be before classes resume?" asked Gramps.

He was asking Uncle Nat, not me, and I was willing to let him answer.

"The School Board is already working on it," Uncle Nat assured him. "They hope they'll have another teacher in the classroom within a week."

Gramps cleared his throat.

"It's not the time factor that bothers me," he stated. "It's the quality of the replacement."

All eyes turned to Gramps.

"Meanin'?" asked Grandpa.

"Well, I don't want to be borrowing trouble—but any teacher worth his salt would already be placed for this school year, as I see it."

I hadn't thought of that, and I guess the others hadn't either, for I saw a few worried looks flicker across the faces around the room.

"We'll just have to pray," stated Aunt Lou. "If there's a fault in the teacher they find, then we'll ask the Lord to change her or him," and she moved to put another stick of wood in the firebox as though everything was now neatly cared for.

"It'll be nice to have you home for a bit, Boy," Grandpa said to me.

"Maybe we can get in some fishing," put in Gramps, his eyes twinkling at the thought.

I nodded. "I'd like that," I stated honestly.

"Josh has some big plans," Nat said slowly, his eyes on my face to read if I wanted him to bring up the subject or not.

I nodded slightly so he would know I wanted him to continue. He caught it and cleared his throat to get all the eyes in the room back on him again.

"Sounds like a good idea to me," Uncle Nat went on. He waited a moment until he was sure everyone was waiting to hear the plan.

"Josh and some of his friends thought this would be a

good time for them to take a little hike up along the creek and spend a few days camping at the spring that feeds it."

Before anyone could even open their mouth to respond, Uncle Nat went on. "Sounds to me like it would be a good experience for the boys. They haven't had much chance for camping with the usual fall bringing all kinds of farm work right along with the good weather. Now this fall is different. The good weather has managed to stay right on even after the fall work is all done. Good time for a boy to take a trip on his own."

Uncle Nat stopped then and all eyes turned back to me.

Before anyone was able to make some kind of response, Aunt Lou made a dash for the stove where the coffeepot was just about to boil over. The eyes shifted off my face, and I silently thanked the boiling coffee and squirmed some on my chair.

Aunt Lou filled coffee cups for the menfolk and went about slicing some of her lemon cake.

It seemed much easier to discuss my plans over coffee and cake and my own brimming glass of Bossie's fresh, cool milk.

"Didn't realize ya had interests in campin', Boy," remarked Grandpa.

"Well, I hadn't thought much on it, there being no proper time and all, so it just didn't come to mind. It was Avery who suggested it," I stated honestly. "Like Uncle Nat said, the time's been too busy when the weather's been good enough."

Grandpa nodded.

"Who ya got to go with ya?" asked Grandpa.

"Avery, Willie and Jack," I answered.

"I mean for grown folk," explained Grandpa.

I hesitated. I didn't know just how to answer. I didn't want to sound sassy or nothing, but I wanted to let him know that boys of fifteen didn't need anyone more grown up than that.

"Well—ah—we—" I started but Gramps cut in.

"I reckon a boy who can pitch bundles like a man and shovel grain to keep up to a threshing machine might be about big enough to care for himself," he said matter-of-factly with a twinkle in his eye.

It was Aunt Lou whose face showed the most concern, though Grandpa didn't look convinced yet either.

"Where'll you eat?" Aunt Lou asked.

"Outdoors," I answered. "We'll take along the food and fix it over an open fire."

Aunt Lou started to speak again, but I saw Uncle Nat quietly reach out and press her hand. No one else noticed. Aunt Lou slowly closed her mouth again and clasped Uncle Nat's hand firmly.

"What do you think?" Grandpa surprised me by asking the question of Uncle Charlie.

Uncle Charlie took a long swallow of hot coffee, let his chair legs drop to the kitchen floor again, and answered without wavering. "S'pose it'd be all right."

I was sure then that I had won. I wanted to whoop but I didn't dare.

"I'll give you a hand with the food, Josh," Aunt Lou offered, and then she checked Uncle Nat's face again to see if he'd consider that interference. A slight flush coloring her cheek, "That is, if you'd like me to," she finished quickly.

"I'd 'preciate it," I hastened to inform her. "Me and the boys were hard put to know what to take along, us never havin' done any campin' or much cookin' before an' all."

"The boys and I," Aunt Lou corrected me, but her smile took any sting out of the words.

It seemed to be settled. Grandpa never did really say yes—but he never said no either. After further discussion, it was decided that we could hike up to the spring on one day, spend three nights camped by the small pool at its base, and then return home on the fourth day. Before I knew what was happening all five people around that table were busy planning what I'd need to take along on that camping trip. By the way their list was growing, it sounded to me like I'd need me a wagon to be hauling it all.

Oh, well! They all meant well. I'd sorta do some sorting through the list myself after they'd had their fun. In the meantime I'd have to get word back to town to the other fellas. We needed to get ourselves going and out on that trip before the School Board announced they'd found us another teacher.

Chapter 4

Off Camping

I don't know who was most excited that morning two days later when the three of us hoisted packs on our backs and started off down the trail that led to the crik.

As it turned out, Jack was unable to join us. We all felt rather sorry for him. His pa had said a determined no—Jack had to stay home and stick to his studies if he was going to be ready for medical school. Jack had been just about sick over it all and, knowing how I'd felt if I'd had to stay home, I felt a little sick myself.

So it was that Avery, Willie and me packed our gear, with a lot of help and advice and instructions from our families, and started down the tree-lined path to the crik. I had only one other regret besides Jack's not getting to go—I had to leave Pixie behind. After talking it over with the three menfolk, I just didn't feel like a campsite was a fit place for a tiny little dog like her, and I knew she'd never be able to walk as far as we were planning on walking. With my arms needing to be free and my back loaded down, I knew I'd never be able to carry her either.

Just before we disappeared from view of our yard, I turned for one more wave. There stood Grandpa, Uncle Charlie, Gramps, and even Uncle Nat and Aunt Lou—they came back out to the farm after the weekend because she didn't want to miss out on any of the excitement—still watching us go. I even saw Aunt Lou blow her nose on her white hankie. You would think we were marching off to war or something. They all looked glad and sad at the same time—happy we were doing something we really wanted to do, and anxious that everything would go alright, and a bit sad that we were growing up.

We three were feeling anything but sad, though, as we stepped out briskly, hardly able to wait until we got out of sight of everyone so we'd truly feel we were on our own.

Our steps slowed down soon enough as the morning wore on. The packs on our backs were feeling a mite heavy and the sun was getting a little warm. It wasn't so good underfoot when we left the worn cow path either. The willow shrubs grew right down to the crik bank, and we sorta had to fight our way through them. We didn't want to leave the bank for fear we'd lose track of the crik among all the trees, so we just kept pushing our way through brush and briar.

I think we all breathed a sigh of relief when we began to see clearing ahead of us and realized the crik was taking us out through the brush and across Turley's cow pasture. The walking would be much easier.

We had just crawled through the fence and were ready for a better path when Avery groaned real loud, stopped and leaned against a fence post.

"I say it's time for a break," he stated. Even though Willie and me were still in a big hurry, I guess we were both getting kinda tired, too.

"We'll rest when we get across the pasture," Willie stated, but Avery didn't even budge.

"I'm resting now," Avery informed us, and we knew it was useless to argue. Avery slid the heavy pack from his shoulders and sat down with his back against it. Secretly I wondered how he'd ever make it all the way to the crik mouth if he was already played out, but I said nothing. Fact is, I didn't mind the idea of a bit of rest myself.

It hadn't been long since Aunt Lou had stuffed us with bacon, eggs and fried potatoes, but Avery seemed to have forgotten that. He reached in his pack and pulled out a handful of Aunt Lou's cookies. Willie and me didn't want to miss out, so we each took a handful, too. The rest, the cookies, and a drink from the crik seemed to refresh us and after several minutes I began to get impatient again. I knew Willie was too, so we suggested to Avery that it might be time to move on again. By my calculation, we'd come only a couple miles and we still had a good piece to go.

Rather reluctantly, Avery picked up his heavy backpack and tugged the straps on his shoulders. Willie and me both picked up ours, shrugged our way into them, and then started off again, me leading the way on account of being the most familiar with the area. It was much easier walking now. Not only were we out of the heavy brush, but the pastureland had been eaten close by the grazing cattle so even the grass was nice and short.

The herd of cattle belonging to the Turleys was feeding nearby, but we paid them no heed except to notice how nice and fat they were and how round their red sides looked.

We had almost reached the other side of the pasture when we heard the awfullest commotion! It sounded like a stampede—and heading our way, too!

I guess we all wheeled around at the sound, expecting to see that whole herd of cows headed right for us.

It wasn't the whole herd—but it might as well have been, for there, coming straight for us, his head lowered and his nostrils snorting out little puffs that blew up tiny clouds of dust, came Turleys' big red bull. Say, if you ever wanted to see three fellas move in a hurry, you would've seen it then. We forgot all about our heavy packs and how tired we were. We just lit out for the closest fence as fast as our legs could take us.

I guess I got there first. I didn't even slow down, but just dropped to the ground and rolled right under that barb wire with one quick motion—pack and all. I heard a sickening tear-sound, and I knew I had ripped the piece of burlap that Aunt Lou had carefully wrapped my pack in. I felt bad about that, but I was powerful happy to be on the other side of the fence from that bull.

Willie whipped under the fence next and rolled right into me. I guess it was then that both of us looked back to see how Avery was faring.

Boy, were we scared! Avery was heading for the fence as fast as his legs could carry him, but he never had been too athletic or nothing, and that bull seemed to be gaining every stride.

"Drop your pack!" I hollered without even stopping to think. If I had, I might have decided that Avery would probably spend more time trying to free himself of that pack than he would save by being rid of it.

Somehow he managed to get his pack off his back and let it fall while he still kept a-running. It might have been his undoing had not that bull taken a sudden interest in that pack. He stopped chasing Avery and stood there pawing and snorting, and then he charged Avery's dumped load as it lay there on the ground. He hit it with an awful smack and wasn't content with that. He sorta ground his horns into it, then hooked it and tossed it up. When it came down he pawed at it again with a sharp hoof, then threw it back into the air, snorting and puffing and carrying on something awful.

In the meantime Avery scrambled under the fence to join Willie and me, panting and puffing and deathly white. I felt a little white myself. Especially when I saw how that bull used that pack Avery had left behind. I was sorry to see Avery's bundle being pawed and pushed right into the ground, but I was sure glad it wasn't Avery.

We lay there trying to collect our wits and quiet our breathing. First I guess we were all just happy to be alive. Then we began to worry some about our supplies.

We had divided our stuff as evenly as we could. I had my bedding, our pots and pans, dishes and cutlery and my fishing gear. Willie had his blankets, a hatchet for cutting firewood, our matches, a first-aid kit and some of our food supplies. Avery had his blankets and most of the food. So with big eyes and sick stomachs, we lay there watching that bull making a big mess of things.

"Scrambled eggs," whispered Willie, a twinkle in his eye in spite of our predicament.

"Sh-h," Avery hissed, his eye on the bull. "You might make him mad."

"Mad?" It was my turn to whisper. "He's mad now."

"Well, madder then," responded Avery.

"Don't see how he could get any madder," I insisted. "Look at him rip things up."

There was nothing we could do about it. We had to lay there and watch that bull have his fun until he decided he had done all the damage he cared to. He left off worrying the pack and came over near the fence and glared at us, still snorting and fuming. We were ready to run, but the scrubby bushes nearby would offer scant protection from this beast. I told the fellas to lay stock-still so we wouldn't rouse that bull up none, and we just held our breath and waited. We sure hoped with all our hearts that the mad bull wouldn't decide to challenge the barbed-wire fence that separated us from him.

Finally the bull wearied of standing there snorting, and he turned and went back toward the cows, bellowing and blowing as he went. He didn't go far though, and every once in a while he circled back our way and snorted at us again just to remind us that he still knew we were there.

We couldn't go on. Not without Avery's pack—or what there was left of it. We hoped at least the food Aunt Lou had packed in tins would still be okay and we would be able to salvage enough to make it through the next three days.

There was no way we could get back into the pasture with that bull still snorting around, so we just moved away from the fence a ways and sat down to wait.

Not much of a way to spend one's camping time. The sun climbed up in the sky and got even hotter and there wasn't a speck of shade. I propped my pack end-up as high as I could and tried to at least get my face out of the sun.

We were all getting awfully thirsty and hungry by the time the sun moved toward the west.

"You've got *some* food, right?" I asked Willie.

He shifted his pack around so he could get into it. It had been tied and wrapped carefully, so it wasn't easy to find the food items without disturbing everything. It had been packed to stay secure until we reached our campsite.

Willie found a loaf of bread and I dug a bread knife out of my bundle. We sliced the bread in rather thick, crooked slices and passed them around. We didn't have even the cheese we had joked about.

By late afternoon the sun was really warm. I had to shift my bit of shade several times. I think I dozed off now and then. Guess Willie and Avery did, too.

When I woke up and pulled myself into a sitting position, that bull was back at the pack again. I had hoped by now the cows might have led him clear across the pasture. They hadn't. He still sniffed and snorted but he didn't work the bundle over anymore.

"We'll never make it to the campsite by dark," grumbled Avery.

"I'm just hoping he left us something to eat," remarked Willie. "We can camp here for the night if we have to and go on in the mornin', but it sure will be a miserable night iffen we don't have somethin' more'n bread for supper."

I agreed.

We were about to give up on that bull ever leaving when the cows decided it was time to head for the barn for milking. The bull looked over at us, snorted again and started off after them.

We let him go a good distance before we even got near the fence. Even then Avery wouldn't crawl through. He had himself too big a scare.

I was the one who went for the pack. It took a bit of doing to gather everything up and bundle it together well enough so I could get the whole thing carried to the other side of the fence.

Avery's blankets had some holes in them and they had been rolled in the dirt in first-rate style, but other than that, they looked fairly usable. The food was another matter. The tins were all dented and some had popped their lids—dust and dried grass were all mixed in with the contents. There was only one egg in the whole dozen that wasn't smashed to bits, and we wondered how in the world it had escaped.

A few things were still edible, and we figured we'd at least have us enough food for our supper. We were all pretty hungry, so we busied ourselves with rustling up some kind of a meal. We blew the leaves and dirt off Aunt Lou's corn bread, covered it with butter, and chowed it all down with some beef jerky Grandpa had sent along. It was already getting dark, it being so late in the fall, and we knew we'd have to give up any idea of traveling on.

There wasn't any shelter to spread our blankets under, either, so we just did the best we could right out in the open.

"Boy, am I tired," sighed Avery. I was too, though *why* I was escaped me. We had walked only a couple of miles and spent the rest of the day dozing there in the sun.

"We'll have to get up early and get on to the campsite," said Willie. "We don't want to lose another day."

Avery pulled off his shoes and started to peal off his pants.

"Whatcha doin'?" Willie demanded. "Ya don't undress when you're campin'."

Avery shrugged, pulled his pants back on again and crawled under his dusty blankets.

By morning I think all of us were right happy for every stitch of clothes we were wearing. In spite of the blankets, it was cold out in the open. A glaze of frost covered the grass around us and I wondered if there might be a bit of it covering my nose as well.

We didn't dare build a fire. The stubble grass around us was too flammable. Besides, we had no wood anyway, so we just sliced off some more bread and ate it with Aunt Lou's cold beans. It was some kind of drink we missed the most. Aunt Lou had tried to talk us into bringing milk, but we insisted that it would mean more to carry and our loads were heavy enough as it was. We'd have the cold, sweet spring water, we assured her. Well, we would've too if it hadn't been for that old red bull.

We wrapped up our packs the best we could, shivering while we did so, and started out for our campsite before the sun had even crawled over the eastern horizon.

Chapter 5

The Campsite

I guess all three of us were pretty anxious to wend our way up the crik. None of us had ever been there before, but we had all heard from folks who had seen the spot where the spring water bubbled out from the hillside on its way to the farmlands below. They all said what a swell spot it was with the water as clear and cold as ice crystals. The green trees leaned over the small pond "like they was tryin' to reach their fingers down to the water," said Grandpa.

With a long ways still to hike, we hurried as best we could—some of the hike was fairly easy, some a little harder, and some of it was downright tough. We fought our way through bush and swampy areas, always hanging close to the crik bank. There were a couple of times when we could have left the crik and taken an easier route, 'cause we knew right well which way to head and all and when we would be joining up with the crik again. But I guess we all three were pretending we were in a brand-new country, one we'd never seen before, and if we didn't hang in tight to that crik, we'd get us lost for sure.

We stopped for some bread and cheese and a couple big juicy apples (they'd been in Willie's pack) about noon. When we started off again, Willie wasn't talking much and I could see him studying everything around us with a sort of contented smile on his face. He sure was enjoying this hike all right, even though he did have the heaviest pack. He had stuffed some of Avery's broken load in his already overflowing sack. I knew he had more than his share to carry but he didn't complain.

Avery more than made up for Willie's quiet though—and all of it was complaining. I began to wish it'd been Avery 'stead of Jack who'd stayed home, even if the trip had been his idea. Willie didn't take no notice of Avery. He seemed to be totally taken with the woods, the crik, and the birds that were staying for the winter.

It was afternoon and we were all sure we must be getting near the mouth of our stream. We came around a bend in the crik right smack into a steep cliff in the hillside. We had traveled the whole time on the north side of the crik, and now it cut into the hill so there was no room to walk. We'd have to cross the crik and follow on the south side for at least the present.

The crik was not deep, nor was it wide, but there was no way we could jump across it. There were no steppingstones either, and that meant getting wet. I was preparing to take off my shoes and socks and roll up my pant legs for wading when Willie spoke up.

" 'Member that fallen log, just back a piece?"

Avery and I both looked at him. I hadn't seen any fallen log, but then I hadn't been watching as closely as Willie. I had likely been distracted by Avery's grumping. Since Willie paid him no mind, Avery had stuck with me.

"I didn't see no log," said Avery shortly.

"Just a couple hundred yards back or so," insisted Willie. "I'm sure it was put there for a crossing. It stretched right from the one bank to the other. If we go back, it'll save us gettin' our feet wet. Even though it feels hot enough, that water'll be cold, and we won't have much chance to warm up none—with night comin' so early and cool."

It made sense to me. I wasn't too anxious to have another miserable night with cold, damp feet to boot.

"Sure," I said, "iffen you saw a log to cross over on, let's go back to it. I'm not hankerin' for cold feet all night either."

"We should've crossed in the first place," groused Avery, "an' saved ourselves all this extra travelin'. This pack is heavy enough without totin' it fore and back."

I gave Avery a disgusted look. His pack, thanks to his throwing things to the bull and getting them all broke up and then palming his leavings off on Willie, was the lightest of the three. I didn't say so though, just turned and followed Willie back down the path.

Willie was right. The log was right there where he'd said it would be, from one side to the other. I daydreamed about other shoe prints on it, feet other than ours that had crossed over before us—maybe even Indians! Maybe they were the ones who'd put the log there. It was sort of like being an explorer or pioneer or something.

Willie went first. He crossed that log slick as you please. You woulda thought he'd been practicing all his life. But, then, Willie was never one to be scared of things. He'd always been the first one to take a dare—walking a high board fence, or climbing the pasture spruce trees, or most anything. I'd noticed that since he'd invited God into his life, he wasn't so apt to do crazy things that were actually dangerous just for the fun of it.

I was next over. I wasn't quite as sure of myself as Willie had been. I tried not to let it show, but every step I took I thought I'd be feeling that cold water washing over me.

Avery hollered after me, "Hey, wait for me, Josh! My shoes ain't made for scalin' slippery-barked trees. I'll never make it with this heavy pack an' all."

I couldn't turn around to look at Avery and I sure couldn't stop in the middle of that log with nothing to hang on to.

"You can make it iffen we can," I called back over my shoulder.

Avery didn't say any more and I could feel him step up onto the log and start working his way across. I still couldn't turn to look. It took all my concentration just making it myself.

I was just stepping onto the bank and heaving an inward sigh when I heard this awful screeching sound behind me. I

turned around just in time to see—you've guessed right—
Avery teetering back and forth, trying hard to regain his
balance. But you could see he was losing out. Finally, with
a shout for help he slipped off the log, still grabbing for a
hold that wasn't there, and fell with a big splash right into
the crik.

For a moment I thought I heard the crik giggling—but I
guess it was just a gurgle as Avery slipped under and then
came up again.

The water was only past his knees when he finally struggled to a standing position, but deep or not, it had thoroughly
soaked Avery. He stood there with the water running off him,
sputtering and wiping his face. His eyes looked scared—or
angry; I couldn't tell which—and the clothes stuck close like
the feathers on a rooster that has been chosen for dinner and
dipped in water for plucking. Boy, did I want to laugh. I didn't
dare even exchange looks with Willie. I knew what would
happen if I did, and Avery already looked upset enough.

And then I noticed Avery's pack. It was still sitting there
in the water, and in it was a good portion of what was left of
our food supply. Boy, if we ever went camping again, Avery
would be the one carrying the pots and pans, I decided right
then. He probably couldn't do much harm to iron skillets and
enamel pots.

Willie must've thought of that food at the same time I
did, for he swished past me, throwing off his own backpack
as he ran, and was in that there crik and scooping out the
soaking pack. Willie hadn't stopped even to take off his shoes
or socks and roll up his pant legs.

Most of the damage had already been done. Willie and I
groaned as we sorted out soggy bread, cookies, and dripping
bacon. The crik-washed vegetables and fruit were okay. A
few things were still protected in the tins Aunt Lou had
packed and the bull had dented. Still, we for sure had lost a
fair amount of our provisions for the days ahead. Made me
feel a little sick inside.

Avery's blankets were all wet, too, and so were his extra
clothes. Wouldn't help none for him to slip behind a bush and

change. What he already had on was just as dry as anything we pulled out of his pack.

Surprisingly, Avery hadn't said one word since he dragged himself out of the crik and stood shivering on the shore. Willie reached in his own pack and came up with some dry clothes.

"You'd better get outta your wet things before you catch a chill," he said, and without comment Avery took the dry clothes and headed behind a nearby scrub bush.

"What're we gonna do now?" I whispered to Willie when I thought Avery was out of earshot.

"Not many choices," Willie whispered back. "We've got to set up camp as soon as possible and try to get Avery's stuff dried out."

I nodded, but I sure did hate to stop when we must be so close to the spring.

I slowly pulled myself to my feet. "I'll get some wood for a fire," I sighed.

When I got back with the wood, Willie had spread all of Avery's clothes and blankets on the nearby bushes to dry, and he was trying to make some kind of sense out of our food supply. I could tell he was thinking of supper. He likely was as hungry as I.

I scraped away dry leaves until I reached the ground beneath. When I thought I had a safe base for the fire, I scooped handfuls of sand from the crik bank onto the spot and then went to work arranging dry leaves and grass and small chunks of wood. The fire started as soon as I put a match to it, and I think all of us greeted that cheery glow with thanks. Avery crowded in close, a mournful look on his face, almost before I had time to get myself out of the way.

As soon as the fire was going good enough, we whipped out a frying pan and put some bacon to sizzling. Boy, did it smell good. We still had some of Aunt Lou's beans, so we warmed them in a pot. We weren't sure if the crik water was pure enough to drink here, so we dipped out a can of it and put that on to boil. It was hard to get all three things to stay upright over the flame, and it took Willie and I our full time and attention to sort of keep moving things around and shoving sticks under and all. Avery just sat there and shivered.

"We'll have to plan on beddin' down here for tonight," Willie informed us. "We can put up a shelter in the trees in no time and keep a fire goin' all night iffen we have to."

I knew that meant a lot more wood, so I picked up the hatchet and went off to get some stacked up. Willie stayed near enough to the fire so he could rescue anything that started to burn; then he started piling up some tree branches against a leaned-over tree so a shelter would be formed.

Avery was the one to call us for supper. Guess he had just been sitting there near to the fire and smelling the food till he couldn't stand it anymore. We got our plates and dished up the beans and bacon, Willie making sure the portions were divided evenly. Then I stirred cocoa mixture into the bubbling water and poured out the hot liquid into our three tin cups. It sure would help to warm up our cold bodies. Willie and Avery were without shoes, them both having waded in the crik water. I had shared my extra socks with Willie, but none of us had brought extra shoes along.

The food sure tasted good. We could hardly wait till Willie had said a short grace. Then we tore into it like it was a fancy banquet or something. They say the outdoors makes things taste even better. Maybe. All I know is that supper sure did taste good. The only fault with it was that there wasn't enough. And we sure did miss bread. Guess all of us were still hungry when our plates were cleaned up.

We each had a fall pear and felt sorrowful about not having some of Aunt Lou's man-sized sugar cookies to go with it, but not one of us found the soggy mess that had been cookies too appealing.

The sun was already dipping around to the west. We knew it wasn't really late, but it was beginning to get cool. Without none of us saying so, I guess we decided the day had been long enough.

I was the only one with shoes, so I kept on hauling in the wood supply. I was sure I had far more than we would ever need, but it did seem to be important to have enough to keep us warm, so I just kept piling it higher and higher.

Willie and Avery kept putting branches up against the lean-to shelter. Then they put some more branches on the ground until they had a nice, thick mattress of sorts. Willie got out our blanket supply then. When I came in with a load of wood, he was busy making up one bed. I must have frowned or something because Willie seemed to think he owed me some kind of explanation.

"Only hope we have of stayin' warm with just two sets of blankets is to all three sleep together."

I supposed he was right, but I wasn't used to sharing a bed with anybody. I didn't think it would bother Willie much. He'd been sleeping with two brothers for about as long as he could remember.

We fed the fire, washed up our dishes and put away the remaining food supply. I wondered just how many meals it would make. I was glad I'd brought my fishing gear.

None of us undressed. I slipped off my shoes and set them under the shelter in case it should decide to rain in the night. Willie and Avery both put their shoes as close to the fire as they dared, hoping they would be dry enough to wear come morning.

Then we all crawled into the shelter and settled ourselves in our bed. It was decided that since Avery was the most chilled, he would sleep closest to the fire. And it would be his job to keep it stoked during the night.

Willie was the most used to sleeping with someone else, so he elected to sleep in the middle. I had the spot at the back—away from the fire and toward the stacked tree limbs that made our shelter.

It wasn't the best night I have ever spent, I can tell you that. The prickly little spikes of spruce needles poking up through the blankets scratched you in places where you didn't need or want to be scratched. The branches on the tree limbs, at the back of the shelter kept swiping at my face every time I moved or even breathed. Avery hogged the blankets, even if he was the closest to the fire. He seemed to roll himself in them, and I hardly had enough at the back to reach around myself.

I slept fitfully. Willie wasn't as good about sleeping in the middle as I had thought he would be. He kept twisting this way and that, and in our cramped quarters there just wasn't room for twisting. Avery slept. In fact, he slept so well he never did replenish the fire, and it was stone cold before it could do us much good. Come morning we were all shivering, the shoes were still soupy wet, and the stack of wood was just as high as it had been the night before.

We woke up grumpy and stiff before the sun was even in the sky. I fought my way out from the tree branches at the back and over Willie and Avery, pulled on my cold shoes and started to work on another fire, my fingers feeling stiff and icy as I tried to hold the matches steady.

I found the beat-up tin that Aunt Lou had filled with pancake fixings, added some crik water to the dry ingredients and poured some of the dough into the frying pan even before it was heated enough to sizzle. They didn't turn out too well—least not those first ones. They were still pale and soggy and wouldn't flip worth nothing, but we ate them anyway. They weren't too bad with maple syrup poured over them. By the time I got to the end of the batch, the pan was too hot and they were burning even before they got a chance to cook.

In spite of all that, they tasted so good I whipped up another batch and we ate them, too. That finished off our pancake fixings. What Aunt Lou had thought would feed us for three breakfasts, we had managed to polish off in one. But then, we reasoned, we hadn't eaten too well the day before.

The crik-drowned shoes were still wet, and the clothes and blankets in need of more drying time, so we knew it would be foolish to break up camp yet. We decided to stay right where we were.

"We have to stay here and get dried out," said Willie. "We only have one more night to stay. There is just no way we can get up in the mornin', walk the rest of the way to the spring and then get all the way back home again in one day."

"You mean we have to turn around from here and go on home without even seein' the spring we came all this way to see?" moaned Avery.

"Well, I'm sure not tryin' to walk on to that spring in my bare feet," said Willie. "You wantin' to?"

Now I knew Avery had never gone barefoot in the summer months like I had done for many summers. But I knew right well if it came down to seeing or missing that spring, I sure wouldn't have hesitated to go shoeless, even if it was the fall and even if there wasn't a decent path through the bush, but I didn't say anything.

"Doesn't seem fair," grumbled Avery. "Here we were tellin' all the fellas how we were gonna hike to the spring, and now we hafta go home and say we didn't see the spring at all."

I was feeling pretty low myself.

"Josh can still go—he's got shoes," Willie suddenly cut in.

Now I hadn't even thought of going on all alone. But when Willie seemed so excited and Avery's eyes lit up, I suddenly felt great relief. I would get to see the spring after all.

I knew this wasn't the way we had planned it, but it did seem better than nothing. At least one of us would be able to report to the other fellas what the spring looked like in the fall of the year.

We decided I would venture up the crik on my own while the fellas dried out their clothes at our camp. I knew Willie and Avery hated to miss the adventure and I felt real sorry for them, but there didn't seem to be much point in my just sitting with them by the fire.

I carried more wood before I left, and they snuggled back under the blankets. I knew that with nothing better to do, they would catch up on the sleep they had missed the night before. It was all I could do to keep my eyes open. I guessed I had missed more sleep than either of them.

Still I felt excitement urging me on. I was anxious to see the place where our crik was born. Was it really as pretty as folks said? Was the water as pure and cold? I decided to take a pail along with me so that when I found it, I could bring some of that famed water back to the fellas.

Chapter 6

The Spring

Though truly excited, as I explained before, I was also disappointed when I realized I would be going on up the crik by myself. I don't know if my disappointment was for myself or for the other fellas. I know they felt bad about having to stay at the campsite while their shoes dried out. But, too, it wouldn't be quite the same not having anyone to share the hiking experience with.

I started up the trail just a bit downcast. But I hadn't gone far when my spirits began to lift. The sun was warm and bright—who could be gloomy with all this sunshine around? A breeze rustled the leaves that stubbornly still hung on to the tree branches. Twittering birds flitted back and forth above me. In spite of the warm weather, most of the migrating birds had already left us, but I saw noisy jays and flirting chickadees, and such. I even saw a large hawk sitting on a tree stump, his preened feathers glistening in the sun.

As I said, I don't know who could have stayed feeling down on such a day. I was walking through one of the prettiest parts of the countryside I had ever seen. I had never been this far up the crik before, and I sure was enjoying the sight now.

I had no idea how far I would have to walk before coming to the spring. Maybe an hour or two? But the deeper I got into the heavy tree growth along the crik, the less I was concerned about the distance. I was just sauntering along, looking all around me at the prettiness of God's creation and thinking of how Gramps would enjoy it all if he could be there with me.

It seemed like no time until I heard a sound like falling water, and I hurried forward. I pushed my way through the trees and along the crik bank and, rounding the bend in the stream, I caught my breath with the sight before me.

There on the steep slope of a hill was a pretty little waterfall. As my eyes traveled up it to where it came out of the rocks above, I realized this was the spring—the beginning of our crik. I just stood there staring as the silvery water caught the sunlight and danced on down to the shallow pool directly beneath it, cool and clean. It was like they said—all around the pool the long, fingery tree branches seemed to stretch downward to reach toward the sparkling water. Here and there a dark spruce or pine shadowed the lighter greenery, and small shrubbery, still dressed in autumn reds and golds, looked at themselves in the mirror waters. It was a sight the like of which I'd never seen before. I just stood there, filling my eyes and my soul with it.

At last I let out my breath and moved slowly forward. I knelt at the side of the pool and eased one hand down into the water. It was so cold my fingers soon began to tingle.

I dropped down in the mossy carpet covering the bank and let my eyes travel every inch of the area and then slowly back again. I don't know just how long I sat there, drinking it all in. I finally roused myself with a sigh, then pulled myself to my feet and began exploring the ground all around the little pond.

Boy, I was sorry the other fellas weren't with me! They were really missing something, all right.

Reluctant at the thought of leaving this place, I dipped my pail in the coolness of the pond water so that I could hurry some back to the boys. Then I had another idea and let the water slip from the pail back into the pool again. I moved back around the small pool and climbed up the rocks to where the spring came out of the hillside.

This is why they call it a spring, I mused. *It does "spring" right out of that rock.*

By stretching the pail as far as I could, I managed to reach the silver stream of water that tumbled down from above. The icy water splashed over my hand as I caught the water in my bucket. I wanted to get it back to the fellas at camp as quick as I could so it would still be cold, but how I hated to leave the place.

"I'll be back," I whispered my promise; "iffen I have my way, I'll sure be back. An' when I come, I'll camp right there by that pool and listen to the song of the waterfall all night long."

I circled the little pool once more and after one last long look, I headed back the way I had come. This time I covered the ground much more quickly.

When I reached our campsite the sun had moved high in the sky and was already heading for the western horizon. I hadn't realized until I got close to the camp and smelled the lingering aroma of food how hungry I was.

When I came hurrying in, hustling that pail of spring water before it had time to become warm in the afternoon sun, both Willie and Avery looked a bit shamefaced. But I was so excited to tell them all about the pool that I didn't really notice it or pay much attention to the fact that the fire had gone out, though I sure was hungry. I went into great detail describing the waterfall, the pool, the surrounding greens and reds and golds. I shoved the pail of water toward them, insisting that they try a cold drink. At great length I told them just how cold it had been when I had started back with it and would have rattled on and on—but my stomach started to rumble. I sure was hungry.

I looked at the blackened kettle over the cold ashes of what had been the campfire, then fell to my knees and reached for the grimy pot.

Willie started to apologize but I waved it aside.

"It's okay," I assured him. "I don't mind eatin' things cold."

"Well—ah—well ah—" muttered Willie. "I'm afraid there isn't anything cold left to eat."

"Then I'll just start the fire again and cook up some more of whatever you had," I offered. "What'd you have?"

"Well—Willie baked potatoes and carrots over the coals," said Avery helpfully.

"Sounds good," I said. "Did it take long?"

But neither of them answered my question.

"We cooked all of the potatoes and carrots that we found," put in Avery after a while. "Even so we were hard put to find enough. Some animal got in our supplies last night. Seems he liked vegetables." Avery was warming to his story. "We had to scout around to find a few things left, and then we had to cut out the teeth marks before we cooked them."

"Oh," I said, then brightened at this idea. "Well, I'll just fry me up some bacon then."

Willie squirmed on the rock he was using for a stool. "Bacon's all gone, too," he said, his voice low and his eyes on the ground.

That slowed me down. I already knew we had no bread, no cheese, no more apples or pears, no cookies or no pancake fixings.

"What is there?" I finally asked the dreaded question.

"Beans," answered Willie and Avery in unison.

"I think I'll catch me a fish," I mumbled, trying hard to keep the disgust out of my voice.

"While you're gone I'll build the fire and heat up the beans," Avery quickly offered. I thanked him for that and got my fishing gear.

Willie looked worried.

"You sure you wanta wait to eat till you've caught a fish?" he inquired. "You know it can take a while to get one iffen they decide not to bite."

I didn't tell him I didn't see where I had much choice.

"I ate an apple 'n pear while I was walkin'," I said instead. "I'll be okay till I get a fish in the pan." With a show of more confidence than I felt, I started off down the trail. I thought

I had spotted a likely place for the fish to hang out about a quarter mile up the crik.

It did take a bit longer than I had hoped to get a fish on the hook. I had to change my location twice before I finally caught something. When I did get a small northern I was pleased with it. My growling inwards were anxious to get it back to camp and into the pan.

As I neared the campsite I could smell something peculiar. I was expecting the rich, savory odor of baked beans to greet me, but this wasn't it.

As I stepped into the small clearing where our lean-to hugged the fallen tree, I looked about me. I could see a lump under the blankets again, and I knew someone was having another nap. It turned out that two someones were bundled in the blankets. The fire was stone cold again, though I could see it had been built up, just like Willie had promised. A blackened pot sat on three stones. I looked in. It was hard to be sure, but I guessed the charred, smelly remains in the bottom of the pot was the last of Aunt Lou's baked beans. I groaned.

It took me some time to get the fire hot enough to get the frying pan sizzling. I was glad we still had some butter and the can of flour, salt and pepper Aunt Lou had sent along for seasoning our fried fish. I cleaned the fish, washed it thoroughly in the cold creek water and then rolled it until it was completely covered with the flour mixture. Then I placed the butter in the sizzling pan and gently dropped the fish pieces into the golden fat. Boy, did it smell good.

For a fella who had only had an apple and a fall pear to tide him over since his breakfast pancakes, I certainly showed some constraint while waiting for that fish to get golden brown. I would have enjoyed some of those baked beans or a slice of bread or something else to go with it, but that sure didn't slow me down none. I lit into that fish before it was even cool enough to swallow.

The smell of the frying fish was hanging pretty thick in the air, and it wasn't long till I saw those fellas began to twitch and turn in their sleep. I heard Willie sort of groan, and I supposed they were hungry again, too. Not that I wasn't a one to share—but, after all, what was one little fish among three fellas? I ate faster.

Sure enough, before I was finished, Avery was crawling up out of the blankets, licking his lips, and Willie wasn't too far behind him.

I sorta kept my back to them and went right on finishing up my fried fish. I figured they were probably about as hungry as I had been. I didn't want to appear selfish or anything, so I half-turned toward them and said around the bite of fish in my mouth, "My pole and hook is there iffen you want to use it."

Avery had never been one for fishing, but he liked eating, so he picked up the pole and, with Willie following, set off down the trail to the crik.

"There's a fair-sized hole about a half mile or so," I called after them. "Seems to be a pretty good one."

After I had finished my supper I washed up my few dishes in the crik, put the pot to soak and went to the lean-to. It seemed it was about my turn to get a little sleep. Especially if we all had to sleep in the same small space again. I sure wasn't looking forward to that, and boy was I tired.

I took off my heavy shoes and placed them carefully under the lean-to, made sure my jacket was fastened up, crawled to the rear of the makeshift shelter and curled up in the blankets. In no time at all I was warm and drowsy. I didn't even hear the fellas come back.

Chapter 7

Return Home

The chill of an autumn morning stirred us from our blankets early the next day and sent us scrambling to build a fire. I had already piled wood beside the makeshift shelter and, after gathering a few dry leaves, some bark and tinder-like grass, we soon had a welcome fire going.

The sun was just pulling itself radiantly from its bed to greet the new day. I thought I could feel excitement in each ray that reached out to send delightful warm shivers along my back and across my shoulders. The sun's warmth joined the campfire in taking the last of the night's chill from our bones.

As soon as we began to thaw, we started to think about eating. We were all hungry but, like I had found out yesterday, there really wasn't much left in our packs to eat. Oh, we had a little butter, some syrup, a mixture of flour, salt and pepper, and a few little things like that. But that didn't sound like a breakfast.

"What're we gonna eat?" asked Avery, mournfully digging through the remains of our camp supplies.

"Guess we'll have to fish," responded Willie.

"We didn't have much luck last night," Avery grumped.

"Didn't you get any?" I asked, realizing then that I had fallen asleep before they had returned.

"Not a nibble," answered Avery shortly. The remembrance of it still irked him.

"Might be biting better this morning," I said as cheerfully as I could.

"Sure hope so," cut in Willie. "I'm near starved."

We picked up my pole and without speaking further headed for the crik. I led the way to the hole where I had been successful the day before, and we settled ourselves down to some serious fishing. Avery remained behind to keep the fire burning and get the frying pan hot.

We sat in silence for many minutes, not wanting to scare the fish and spoil our chances for breakfast.

Then Willie spoke in a whisper, "This trip isn't just what we'd expected, is it?"

I looked at him in silence. I knew it wasn't, but I wasn't sure just how much I was willing to admit—even to myself. Maybe camping wasn't really all it was cracked up to be, anyway.

"Not that I haven't enjoyed it," Willie hurried on, "but you must admit we've sure had our share of bad breaks."

I thought about Avery, my best friend for many years, and how he had sorta botched up a lot of things for us.

"Wasn't Avery's fault." Willie's declaration seemed to answer my thoughts. "Can't really say he's had the best time in the world either. I mean, who'd care to be chased by a bull? And then that dunkin' in the cold crik wasn't exactly fun. He's been just as hungry as the rest of us—and just as disappointed about missin' out on not seein' the spring, too."

I nodded my head in agreement. It had been a rough trip for Avery—and him not even caring too much for the out-of-doors besides.

"I've been thinkin'," Willie said thoughtfully, "maybe God sorta arranged this trip."

I looked up then, square at Willie. Now, where did he ever get an idea like that?

Willie returned my look and his eyes did not waver.

"Did you know that Avery is painin' inside?"

"Avery?"

"Yeah. He never says much—but yesterday when you were gone to the spring, well, we got to talkin' an' Avery opened up an' really said what he was feelin'. You know his mom's been awful sick an' that Avery already lost a brother. I think he wanted this trip to kinda get away and do some thinkin'. He's scared, Josh. He's really scared. He's got this silly notion that God is just out to hurt him or somethin'. He's just sure his mom is gonna die—an' for some reason he thinks it's his fault."

"Avery?" I said again, a little too loud. I checked myself. I sure didn't want to be scaring away our breakfast fish.

"Well, we had a long talk—an' then we prayed together. We gotta help him, Josh. Show him that we're his friends and we'll stick with him. Show him that God really does love *him*."

I nodded again. It sure did give one something to think about all right. If we hadn't had all of our "bad luck," Willie never would've had the chance to talk and pray with Avery like he did. We still wouldn't have known that Avery needed special friendship at this time.

We fished in silence again, but it was no use. The fish just weren't biting. We got up and moved on down the crik and tried another hole, and then another. Still nothing. I was beginning to wonder if maybe God had it in for all three of us.

"We better give up," said Willie. "Iffen we don't get packed up and on our way, we won't make it back home today."

I knew Willie was right but, boy, was my stomach complaining.

We went back to the campsite, and Avery's face, which brightened at our return, quickly fell again when he saw we had no breakfast.

We began to pack up our gear. I was about to throw out the remaining flour mixture when Avery hollered at me.

"Hey!" he yelled. "Don't throw that out. It would make a pancake."

"With pepper in it?"

"It's worth a try," Avery insisted. "I'm so hungry I could eat anything."

But he wasn't. I mean, he took that flour mixture, stirred in the one egg that we'd forgotten we had, added some crik water and fried the flat, rather distasteful-looking thing in butter in our frying pan. It didn't smell so bad as it cooked, but it didn't look too great. Avery then poured what was left of the syrup over it and sat down to have his breakfast. By then Willie and I were wishing we'd spoken up for some as well. But Avery took one bite and spit it clear across the campsite. Guess it wasn't going to be the answer after all.

We finished up our packing in silence. Inwardly I wrestled with the fact that Avery had wasted that last good egg.

Our packs were much lighter now, and we distributed the load as evenly as we could. Aunt Lou's pot still didn't clean up too good after the scorched beans. I was glad she had insisted on sending an old one. It sure was a sorry mess now.

We decided to stay on the south side of the crik rather than try to cross the fallen log again. We knew our way quite well, and we knew that if we followed the crik all the way to the Turleys', the bridge would get us across to our proper side then.

It was another beautiful fall day, and I guess that we could have really enjoyed our hike home had our stomachs not been so empty. As it was, it was a little hard to concentrate on the blue sky and the whispering fall leaves.

It was well past noon when we reached the Turleys and we had already determined to not follow the crik through their pasture. We didn't want an encounter with that bull again.

We were about to go on by their farmstead on the road when Avery stopped us.

"How about we go on in?" he suggested.

"For what?" asked Willie.

I was afraid Avery wanted to tell them about their mean old bull or something, and then they could very well say we had us no business being in their pasture anyway.

"For a drink," responded Avery. "Even a little water would help my stomach some."

We looked at one another and nodded. Maybe some water would help.

As we neared the Turley house I began to wish we hadn't stopped. Wafting out of the kitchen window and down the lane to greet us was the most wonderful smell you could imagine. Mrs. Turley was baking apple pie.

We all looked at one another and our empty stomachs began to grumble even louder. We said nothing, but the expression in our eyes was shared agony.

It was Avery who stepped up to the door and rapped gently. Fourteen-year-old Mary answered and looked rather surprised when she saw all three of us standing there. She just stared at us.

"Who is it, girl?" called Mrs. Turley, and I was sure enough relieved to hear her voice.

"Boys," answered Mary, and I was afraid she was going to close the door on us and go back to her kitchen duties.

"Well, invite them in," instructed Mrs. Turley, and she came through the kitchen and stuck her head out the door so she could see for herself.

"Come in. Come in," she invited us cheerfully, and we followed her into the kitchen. Her blue gingham sleeves were rolled up and there was flour on her hands and apron.

"What can we do for you, boys?" she asked. Mrs. Turley was known in the community as one who did not bother none with beating around the bush.

"We'd like a drink, please," responded Avery without hesitation. "We've been out on a camping trip and we're on our way home. It's powerful hot walking and we just thought that you might be kind enough to let us have a drink."

"Mary, get the boys some cold milk," said Mrs. Turley, and she went back to rolling out piecrust. Now, milk sounded a whole lot better than water.

"Never did care for milk all on its own," Mrs. Turley went on. "Mary, slice them some fresh bread and get out some of that strawberry jam." Mary hurried to carry out the instructions while Mrs. Turley deftly worked with her rolling pin, and we looked at one another like we'd been offered an expenses-paid trip to New York City. About that time I was blessing my best friend Avery for talking us into stopping.

"So you been campin'," remarked Mrs. Turley.

We managed to reply around giant bites of strawberry-jam-covered fresh bread. Mrs. Turley was a great baker.

"Where'd ya go?"

"Up to the crik mouth, ma'am."

"What fer?"

That one caught us a bit off guard. Why had we gone?

"Just to see the spring," said Willie. "We'd never been there."

"Neither've I," said Mrs. Turley, "an' I don't plan to waste no time in goin' way up there either." Then her voice softened and she even smiled. "But, then, I guess young boys with energy to spare don't quite look at things the way a tired ol' woman does."

We didn't quite know how to respond to that one. None of us were eager to refer to Mrs. Turley as a tired old woman while we sat at her kitchen table wolfing down her delicious homemade bread.

"Mary, cut them each another piece," said Mrs. Turley, watching us for a moment, "an' get them some more milk."

"That is mighty delicious, ma'am," said Avery. "We did have us some bad luck and ended up with no breakfast this morning." I held my breath for a moment, but Avery was smarter than I gave him credit for—he said nothing at all about that Turley bull.

"Then you'd best have a piece of apple pie," answered Mrs. Turley, not missing a beat with the smooth action of her rolling pin. "Mary, cut them a piece of that pie in the window. Mind you, be careful now. It's still hot."

"Oh, but—" started Willie, and I kicked him under the table.

"Sure does smell good, ma'am," I cut in quickly.

Mary was generous with her servings and I suddenly gained a new respect for the girl.

The pie was just as good as it had smelled, and we were given more milk to help cool off each bite. Boy, did it hit the spot!

"Mrs. Turley," I said as I washed down the last swallow

with milk, "that was about the best apple pie I ever tasted."

"That's nice to hear," she said matter-of-factly without smiling. "The way my menfolk swallow the food around here, I'm not sure whether it be good or not. They just gulp it down and leave the table."

I supposed Mrs. Turley might not be the only woman with that complaint. I decided then and there to pay a few more compliments to the cook—whoever it might be.

We thanked Mrs. Turley again, paying her lavish compliments on her bread and pie, which eventually left her beaming, and turned back to the dusty road again.

As we left, Willie turned to Mary, who was busy cleaning up after us.

"And thank you, Mary," he said, "for feedin' us an' all."

A bit embarrassed, Avery and I quickly echoed our thanks. Mary gave us a shy smile.

Once back on the road with our stomachs full and our spirits revived, we began to pay more attention to the fall day, pointing out items of interest to one another.

We even started to reminisce about our camping trip. We first discussed all of the good things about it, like the colorful fall leaves, the fact that it hadn't rained, the clarity and freshness of the crik the closer we got to the spring. Then we started discussing the other things that had happened. We passed that old bull in the pasture, and the whole fearful experience came flooding back. But soon we were seeing the funny side of it all, and we laughed and pounded one another on the back and nearly rolled on the ground. Before we realized it we had quite convinced ourselves that our camping trip had been a tremendous success, and we could hardly wait to get home and tell everyone about it. In fact, we decided, there really wasn't one thing about it that we'd change even if we could. Well, maybe enough food for one last breakfast.

Just the same, I was looking forward to a good sleep in my own bed, with no one there to pull off the covers or breathe in my face.

Chapter 8

School Again

I wouldn't willingly have admitted it to anyone, but I was missing school. The local grapevine tried to keep up with the School Board's search. Rumors were always circulating about as to who they had contacted and where he or she was from and when the new teacher might be coming, but the school door stayed closed. I was getting restless, and I guess most of the other students were feeling the same way. Why, I even took to studying my textbooks—in the privacy of my own bedroom, that is.

I spent the time at the farm with the three men. Grandpa kept looking for little jobs to keep us all busy, but there really wasn't too much more that needed to be done before winter set in. Gramps laughingly suggested that we all take up knittin', but Uncle Charlie said that "mendin' was too close to a needle of any kind" for him.

It really hadn't been that long since our teacher had quit—it just seemed like forever.

I rode into town with Grandpa every chance I got and over to Willie's a couple of times, and over to Avery's once. I even visited Mitch Turley, who had quit school as soon as he could talk his folks into it. I knew Mitch wouldn't understand my hankering to be back in the schoolroom again, so I didn't even mention it to him. Instead, I told him all about our hike up along the crik. It sounded better every time we three fellas told it.

Anyway, I was bored. Guess I was sorta getting on the nerves of the men at the farm because one day Grandpa came in and said he was going into town and I might like to pack up my things and go on back to Aunt Lou's. The latest rumor had it that a new teacher was on the way and school might start just anytime.

Well, we had heard that before and it hadn't amounted to anything, but I didn't argue. I packed up my little valise, threw it in the back of the wagon, then went back into the big farm kitchen to tell Gramps and Uncle Charlie goodbye, scooped up Pixie and we started off for town.

"Feel that bite in the wind, Boy?" Gramps said as he turned up his collar. The wind really caught a body all right when you were perched up on the high seat of that wagon. I nodded my head and turned up my own collar.

"Winter might finally be on its way. Don't know when we ever had us a fall like this one."

I nodded again and looked at the trees lining the roadway. The branches were whipping back and forth and the leaves were dancing here and there, as though scurrying about to find the right bed for snuggling down before the snow started falling.

Grandpa clucked to the horses to hurry, and then I saw him look toward the sky.

My eyes followed his, and it sure did look like snow weather all right. I purposely didn't think about the wood it would take for the fires and the extra work in choring. I smiled to myself and thought instead about sliding down snow-covered hills and skating over frozen ponds.

When we got to Aunt Lou's there was no one to answer our light rap on the door. Grandpa walked right on in, like it was our custom when he brought me back to town, sorta halloing as he did.

"Guess Lou is out—" He stopped quick-like when we heard a noise from the bedroom.

Grandpa cocked his head and listened a minute. "Lou?" he called.

"In here, Pa," came the weak answer.

We both walked to the door of Lou's room. She was laying there with flushed cheeks and the blind on the window drawn.

"Ya feeling poorly?" asked Grandpa softly, and I wondered why he even asked. Lou wasn't one to lay around in bed in the middle of the day.

She smiled, but it was kind of fragile-like.

"Not too bad," she answered, "but Doc says I'm to stay here for a couple of days."

Grandpa walked over to Lou's bed. Automatically, it seemed, his big work-calloused hand reached out and rested on Lou's brow.

"You had the doc?" he asked. I knew that fact concerned Grandpa. One did not call the doc just for sniffles or a tummy ache.

"I'm fine, Pa, really I am," Lou assured him quickly. "Why, I really don't feel too sick at all—but Doc says at my age, I best stay in bed. Measles can bring complications."

"Measles?" I guess Grandpa and I both said the word together.

Lou looked just a mite embarrassed.

"Little Sarah Smith had the measles and then her mama got them, too. I took over a couple books and some chicken soup—and—well, I guess I had no business being there. Anyway, I now have the measles and Doc says, 'Stay in bed,' and Nat says, 'Stay in bed,' so—I stay in bed."

By the way she said it, I knew staying in bed was not easy for Aunt Lou.

"You should have sent for us, honey," Grandpa was saying.

"I'm not sick, Pa. Really. I sure didn't need to go trouble someone else over it."

"Well, Josh is here now," said Grandpa. "He's right handy. He can do any running that needs being done. He can cook, too. Charlie's been teaching him a few things since he's been so bored this week."

Lou gave me a smile. "Good to have you back, Josh," she

said. "I've been missing you." I knew it was more than just someone to run her errands. Aunt Lou really did miss me when I was gone—me and Pixie.

I put Pixie in Aunt Lou's outstretched arms and the little dog lay there, her small tongue busy on Aunt Lou's face. For a moment I was scared—could dogs pick up measles? And then I figured likely not and dismissed my fears.

"I'll just put my things in my room," I said.

By the time I was finished unpacking my few belongings, I could hear the kettle singing. Grandpa was busy making Aunt Lou some fresh tea. I'd noticed some laundry on the line when we drove in, so I decided I'd best slip out and get it before that storm arrived. When I had finally untangled the things that were wrapped around the string of wire, my fingers were tingling with the cold. Yep, winter sure was on its way.

Nearing the house, I could hear Aunt Lou laughing. I don't know what story Grandpa was telling her, but they seemed to be enjoying it together. I folded up the wash, enjoying the fresh, outdoorsy smell of it, and put it in the basket. By then the feeling was back in my fingers.

"Josh," called Aunt Lou, "there are cookies in the pan on the table. Mrs. Brown just brought them this morning. Help yourself and bring some in for Pa, please."

"Anything you need before I start hauling wood?" I asked Aunt Lou around the cookie in my mouth as I handed the pan to Grandpa.

"Could you run to the store for some pork chops for our supper?" she asked me. I nodded that I could and pushed the last of the cookie into my mouth so I'd have two free hands to button up my coat.

The butcher shop was always a busy place. Sometimes I had been there when I'd had to wait in line for ten or fifteen minutes. It wasn't my favorite spot. I didn't care for the smell, the mixture of sawdust and fresh meat. I didn't like to look at the cases full of chunks and pieces that used to be someone's cow or hog, either. I would have rather waited outside, but the wind was cold so I stepped in and took my place in line—for once a short one.

The butcher took care of each customer one by one, and when he had handed Mrs. Olaf her brown-wrapped hamburger and marked it on her sheet, he turned to me.

"Howdy, Joshua. I'm supposin' you've heard the good news?"

I hadn't heard any news, good or bad, that I recalled, so I shook my head.

"No, sir," I stated.

"You didn't? Well, boy, yer holiday is 'bout over. The new teacher arrived on today's train."

I guess he'd expected my face to fall or me to start to grumble or something, for he was all ready to laugh a big laugh at my expense. There must have been a little smile that crossed my lips or showed in my eyes or something, 'cause he looked real surprised and then sad, like I'd spoiled his fun or something.

"Ain't ya upset?" he asked me.

"No, sir," I answered honestly.

"Ya like school?" he went on, incredulous.

I was a little slower to answer that one. I mean, I didn't want to be thought strange or something. I swallowed. "I reckon I do," I said.

He shook his head as though to clear it of cobwebs, and then he said a funny thing. "Good for you. Maybe ya won't need to spend yer life standin' over foul-smellin' meat all day."

He handed me my package and turned to enter it on the sheet that he kept for Uncle Nat.

I didn't rightly know what to say, so I just mumbled my "thank you" and pulled open the door. Besides, I was suddenly in a great big hurry to get home. I had real honest-to-goodness news!

When I reached the house out of breath from running against the wind, Uncle Nat had arrived home from the church and was sitting by Aunt Lou, looking relieved to see her obediently in bed and visiting with Grandpa.

"New schoolteacher's here!" I gasped out to all three of them.

"Is she now?" said Grandpa with a smile. "Then the rumor was right this time."

"He," put in Uncle Nat mildly.

We all looked at him.

Grandpa's eyes returned to my red-flushed face.

"When did she get here, Boy?"

"He," said Uncle Nat again.

We seemed to catch his meaning then—at least Grandpa did.

"It's a man?"

"Right," said Uncle Nat.

"How old a fella?" asked Grandpa, and I wondered if he was thinking about whether the new teacher would be able to handle the older boys.

"Near middle age, I expect," responded Uncle Nat.

"Middle age," repeated Grandpa, seeming to ponder the information. "Did he come alone?"

"No, he has a wife and child."

"Child?" This question, too, was from Grandpa.

"A girl," said Uncle Nat, and I immediately dismissed the fact from my mind. If it had been a boy I might have been interested in his age.

"That's nice," Grandpa was saying. "Real nice. You'll be able to get back to yer studies, Boy."

I nodded and then realized I still held the brown-paper-wrapped pork chops in my hands.

Grandpa stood to his feet and gathered up the cups. "I'd best be gettin' on home 'fore that storm strikes," he said. "Josh, did you bring in the milk and butter?"

"Yes, sir," I answered him.

"Then I'd best get a-rollin'. You take care now, Lou, ya hear? Josh is here and he's happy to do yer runnin'."

Lou smiled. "I promise!" she said. "Though I sure don't *feel* sick anymore."

"I've had an awful time keeping her down," remarked Uncle Nat.

"No use takin' chances," Grandpa reminded Aunt Lou. Then he added thoughtfully, "I thought you had the measles when you were just a little tyke."

"Doc says that they were the Red measles," Aunt Lou replied. "These are the German. One is not usually as sick with them, but occasionally there are complications."

"Well, you take care." Grandpa leaned over to plant a kiss on Aunt Lou's cheek, reached out and tussled Pixie's ear, and then turned to me.

"Glad about your school, Boy," he said again with a quick pat on my shoulder.

He turned to Uncle Nat. "Any idea when classes will start?"

"I heard them say next Monday," he replied.

I was rather disappointed about that. It was Wednesday. I'd been hoping that school would take up again the next morning. I was anxious to get a look at that new teacher. I'd never had me a man teacher before.

"Guess he needs a couple days to settle in," Grandpa was saying.

He placed his hand on my shoulder again and gave it a slight squeeze like he always did when we said goodbye, and then he was off. Uncle Nat went out with him.

It was then that I finally delivered the package of pork chops to the kitchen.

Uncle Nat turned to me good-naturedly. "You can have your pick, Josh," he said. "You want to cook supper or haul the wood?"

I didn't hesitate for one minute. "I'll haul the wood," I responded and went to slip out of my good jacket and into my choring coat before leaving the warm kitchen.

The wind sure enough smelled of snow.

Chapter 9

The New Teacher

Over the next few days there was little time for chafing over school to start. With Aunt Lou still confined to her bed and Uncle Nat busy with church duties, I had plenty to keep my hands and mind busy. The first snowstorm came sweeping in too, and that meant more wood and coal to haul. Boy, was it cold! It seemed that Old Man Winter wanted to make up for lost time, all in a day or so—thought we'd had it warm and sunshiny for quite long enough. The snow piled up overnight and the north wind whipped it into little drifts all around the corners of the house. I had to shovel my way to the coal shed and the woodpile. It did look awfully pretty out though.

Now and then one of the fellas would drop by with the latest bit of gossip about the new teacher. I couldn't invite anyone in because of the house being in quarantine, so we'd talk through the open window or over the front gate. You'd be surprised how many things were being passed around town about the schoolmaster.

One story said he was running from the law, and another one said, no not the law, but the army, and still another said he wasn't running at all but it was his wife who was on the run. Then there were those stories that said he'd been put out of his last school for beating a boy to within an inch of his life, and another that he had lost his school because of some jealous woman who falsely accused him because he wouldn't leave his wife for her.

There were even stories about his finances. Some said he was only a step ahead of creditors, and others said he had lost his home, his horse and his holdings to the town banker where he had last taught.

Nobody seemed to know for sure where he had taught. Nobody seemed to know many *facts* at all, but the gossip kept sweeping over the gates and into the homes of the town folk. Uncle Nat was getting right put out about it all and said that someone should call a town meeting and put an end to all the foolishness. "A man is innocent until proven guilty," he said.

It was all rather mysterious. I could hardly wait to get my first look at the man. I felt quite confident that when I got that look, I would be able to tell right off just which one of the stories had any basis in fact.

By the time Monday finally rolled around, the doc had let Aunt Lou out of bed. She was right anxious to take over her own house again, and I guess Uncle Nat and I were just as anxious to let her.

My lunch pail in hand, well stocked by Aunt Lou, I left for school with a great feeling of excitement. Avery, Willie, Jack and I had agreed to meet at the corner of Main Street and all go to school together. None of us could live with the thought of one or the other of us fellas getting the first look at that new schoolmaster.

Willie and Avery were already there when I came puffing up. The air was frosty and it hurt one's lungs to run hard on such a morning. My insides felt frozen as I came wheezing up to the fellas.

We had to wait for Jack. The three of us stood there stomping our feet and clapping our hands, trying to keep warm. We were about to give up on Jack and go on to school when he came panting around the corner. His cheeks were red—I just figured it to be the cold wind. Then he grabbed my arm and squeezed it real tight.

"You're not gonna believe this," he said. "I wouldn't have

believed it myself iffen I hadn't seen it with my own eyes."

"Seen what?" asked Willie, and Avery and I both perked our ears up too.

"Well, you know the new teacher moved in over near us."

We waited, wondering what news Jack had that would top the tales we'd already heard.

"Well, on Saturday Ma sent me into town for some eggs and milk, and there she was—comin' right outta their gate."

"Who?" we all said together. "Who?" I know our minds were all busy wondering where this new story was going.

Jack looked at us like we should have known "who" without asking.

"His daughter," he said. "Who else?"

"His daughter!" we all fairly exploded.

"Good grief!" said Avery. "I thought you had some *news*."

"Guess his daughter can come out of her own house iffen she has a mind to," I stated sarcastically and turned away from Jack.

"Come on," chimed in Willie. "Let's get to school before we freeze to death."

Jack looked disappointed. For some reason I failed to understand; he had been so excited over his silly bit of news.

"Wait, fellas," he said as we walked away. "Wait—"

But we didn't even want to hear about it.

Jack tried again. "Why the rush? Don't you want to hear—"

"Why should we care if his kid runs down his walk?" demanded Avery. "Is she weird or somethin'?"

Jack pulled me to a stop and the other fellas turned to look at him.

"You haven't seen her?" asked Jack.

We shook our heads, and I tried to shake off Jack's restraining hand.

"Have ya heard about her?" Jack continued.

"I heard he had a kid," I shrugged.

"Yeah, me, too," said Willie, his expression saying, "So what?" He turned away. "C'mon, let's get in there before that bell rings."

Jack let me go then but he had this funny look on his face.

"I think you boys are in for a big surprise," was all he said.

We looked at Jack like he'd lost his senses.

We pushed our way into the small hallway and shook the snow from our coats before hanging them up on our assigned pegs. I felt myself straining forward, trying to catch a glimpse of that new teacher.

Other students crowded into the entry. We exchanged a few teasing pleasantries with the other fellas and let the girls pass without comment. One or two of them looked our way and giggled a bit. Girls were awfully silly, if you asked me.

There was no way we fellas would have entered the schoolroom before the bell rang. It just wouldn't have looked right, somehow. Yet all of us were so anxious to get a look at the man who would be teaching us for the rest of the school year. From the stories that had been circulating, I didn't know whether he would have a long, curling black mustache and shifty eyes, or horns and a red tail.

Anyway, we were still standing there, straining to look around the door that wasn't opened quite wide enough for us to see into the room, when the other door opened and a gust of winter snow swirled in. Behind the snowflakes was the most beautiful creature we had ever seen. I guess our mouths all dropped open. I mean, there she was just a few feet from us, brushing the snow from a green velvet-looking coat, her cheeks flushed a rosy pink, and blue, blue eyes peering out at us from under a white fluffy hat. She took the hat off to shake the snow from it, and brownish-red curls tumbled down all around her shoulders.

Guess Avery found his voice first.

"Who is that?" I heard his hoarse whisper.

I was too busy just looking.

She glanced again over our way and instead of lowering her eyes and flushing in embarrassment or giggling like the other girls, she gave us a flashing look with just the hint of a teasing smile in it and then she was gone through the door.

"Who was that?" Avery croaked again.

"Oh," said Jack with a real smart-alecky grin, "that's just the teacher's daughter."

"Why didn't you tell us?" asked Avery.

"You weren't interested in the teacher's kid. Remember?"

I gave Jack a withering look and pushed my way past the other boys. The bell hadn't rung yet, but I couldn't wait to see if I was dreaming or what.

I found my way to the desk I considered mine at the back of the room and managed to sit down without stumbling over anyone. My books slid carelessly onto the wooden tabletop in front of me and my eyes traveled over the room.

Sure enough. There she was. She had removed her green coat and was wearing a blue dress that brought out the blue of her eyes. Every eye in the room was on her.

Somewhere a bell rang and through a mental fog I saw other students bringing themselves to attention. A voice at the front of the room was speaking to us. Somehow the words got through to me and I suppose I obeyed the orders I was given.

I read when asked to read—answered when spoken to—worked the sums I was given—took part in a spelling bee—even said "No, sir" and "Yes, sir," and somehow made it through the morning, but my mind sure was on other things.

When we were dismissed for the noon hour, all us older fellas clustered together talking, and a good share of the talk was about the teacher's daughter. I listened but did not take part much. I mean, it seemed sorta crude to be discussing her in such a fashion.

Skeet Williams had Jack Berry by the front of the shirt. "What's her name? What's her name?" he was persisting. Jack had suddenly taken on a swaggering air, knowing he was the only one who had really seen this new girl before classes had begun.

Jack hated to admit it, but he didn't know her name.

"It's Camellia," piped up Andy Johnson, with a measure of authority.

"How do you know?" Jack challenged him, hating to grant any further knowledge of the new girl to anyone but himself.

"The teacher—her pa—called her that. Didn't ya hear him?"

Jack hadn't heard him. I hadn't either. But then, I hadn't heard much the teacher had said that morning.

"Camellia," said Avery in a sort of whisper. "That's a flower, ain't it?"

There were many knowing nods and cute comments. I walked away from it all. The way the fellas were carrying on was almost as bad as girls giggling. I just didn't like the feel of it all.

Avery followed me. I walked over the frozen schoolyard kicking up clumps of roughed-up snow, dried grass and anything at all that showed.

"What's the matter, Josh?" Avery said at my sleeve. "You mad about somethin'?"

"Naw," I said. "I ain't mad."

"You're not gettin' those there measles, are you?"

My head jerked up. "No, I'm fine—what gives ya a silly idea like that anyway?"

"Well, yer so quiet-like. Usually you join right in the funnin'."

"Funnin'!" I said sourly. "Is that what that was?"

Avery looked at me in surprise.

He started to say something back but I cut in, "I mean, it don't seem fair somehow to stand talkin' about—about people with them not even there to defend themselves or nothin'."

"We weren't saying nothin' bad," argued Avery.

"Well—'bad' all depends," I continued. "I mean, iffen she—she's a nice girl, then she might not like a bunch a fellas pickin' her over like that—like she was just somethin' to gawk at or somethin'."

Avery swallowed.

"I mean," I went on, "why don't we just forget that girl and go play Fox and Goose or somethin'?"

"You don't like her much, do you? I mean, what's she done—?"

I looked Avery square in the eye. I wanted to tell him just how dumb he was—but he was my best friend. He flinched some at my look and scuffed his feet back and forth on the solid ground.

"It's got nothin' to do with likin' or not likin'," I finally said. "I don't even know her—yet. Neither do you. Nor do any of those other fellas. But standin' around talkin' about her doesn't do anybody any good. We might as well be playin' or somethin'."

"I'll get the guys," said Avery, but before he turned to go he said one more thing—quiet and almost condemning— "You're gettin' more like your preacher uncle every day, you know that? Ever'body in town knows he won't tolerate nobody talkin' 'bout nobody," and Avery wheeled and was gone.

I knew Uncle Nat didn't care none for town gossip. He had been the butt of it far too much himself as a kid growing up in a difficult situation. But I hadn't known he had a name about town for not allowing it in his presence.

Well, maybe I had learned it from my uncle Nat. I didn't like the feel of gossipy tongues either. And I wasn't one bit ashamed of the fact.

Avery gathered up the fellas and we set us out a ring for Fox and Goose. The game got pretty lively, but I noticed fellas continually casting glances over at the girls' side where the new girl, Camellia, was playing tag.

She fit in real nice and ran about as fast as Mary Turley, who was considered a real good athlete for a girl.

The bell rang and we got to go back into the warm schoolroom. I couldn't help but notice how pretty Camellia was with her cheeks flushed and her coppery hair tousled from running in the wind.

At the close of the day all of us older fellas left the schoolyard together, and you can just guess what the topic of conversation was. But I didn't want to listen to it. It just didn't seem right somehow for them all to be talking about her and laughing and joking and all. I pulled away from the rest of them and said I had to hurry and get home 'cause Aunt Lou might be needing me.

I guess I ran all the way—I don't really remember.

When I came into the warm, fresh-bread-smelling kitchen, Aunt Lou looked just fine.

"So how was your first day back at school, Josh?" she asked me.

I answered, "Fine."

"Was it good to be back?" she questioned.

I said that it was.

"And what is your new teacher really like?"

I started to answer, then stumbled to an embarrassed halt. I suddenly realized that I had no idea. I couldn't even remember what the man looked like.

Chapter 10

The Storm

The next day I made a point of taking a real good look at our new teacher. I didn't want to be caught again in an embarrassing situation like I had with Aunt Lou the night before. If necessary, I would even figure out his shoe size!

His name was Mr. Foggelson, that much I knew. So Camellia's last name would be Foggelson, too. Camellia was an only child. Everyone said she most favored her ma, so I guessed her ma must be a fine-looking woman.

But I was off track again. Back to Mr. Foggelson, our teacher—he was of medium size, neither big nor small. He didn't have a long, black mustache and shifty eyes, and he certainly did not have horns and a tail. He was clean shaven and had blue eyes—well, not real blue like Camellia's but sort of a gray-blue. His hair was medium brown in color, not dark, not light, and it didn't have the rich reddish-brown tones of Camellia's hair. His chin was neither jutting in a stubborn way nor small and lost in his neckline like a mousy man's might be. He was a rather ordinary-looking man.

His voice was well-modulated and even-pitched, neither high nor low. He taught with authority without being overbearing. He seemed to know the subject matter well. He was patient with the slow learners, but seemed to show real appreciation for a good mind. All in all, I had to admit he would probably be the finest teacher I had ever had in my limited years of schooling.

Having carefully made my mental report for Aunt Lou or anyone else who might ask, I went back to letting my thoughts wander to other things—like whether Camellia liked to skate on frozen ponds or toboggan down steep, bumpy hills. I was imagining her with her hair flying in the wind and her cheeks flushed from all the excitement.

I wonder if she'd like to go out to the farm with me? I thought. I was sure Gramps had never seen such a pretty girl and would never believe my description of her.

I wondered if she liked dogs and how she would feel about my Pixie. Somehow I could picture her with Pixie in her arms, running her slim, long fingers through the soft, fluffy fur. I could hardly wait to get the two of them together, sure that it would be instant, mutual love.

Will I stutter and make silly blunders before I even have a chance to show her that I am different than the other fellas? I worried. *That I really do care about her as a person, not just a pretty face?*

And then I realized that "a pretty face" was all I really knew about Camellia. Well, I'd just have to set myself to finding out more about her.

The week rushed by—all too quickly, I thought, filled as it was with daydreams and snatched glances and "chance" encounters. I wondered just how I would manage the whole weekend without even a glimpse of her or anything. Many of my classmates lived right in town and would have the opportunity to see Camellia as she went to the grocer's for her ma, or out for a walk with her pa, or something. Me, I'd be out at the farm with the menfolk—all alone.

I didn't talk to any of my family about Camellia. Not that I wasn't thinking about her some—I just didn't know what to say or how to say it. I tried whispering a few little things to Pixie—and then felt my cheeks get hot with embarrassment.

I got through Saturday, though my mind really wasn't on my farm chores. I was looking forward to Sunday. I was just sure that Camellia and her folks would be at Uncle Nat's church, his being the only church in town. I could hardly wait to have Gramps see her. He'd notice her for sure—I mean, she stood out in a crowd, and then he'd ask me who this new girl was and I'd be able to say, "That's Camellia Foggelson, the daughter of the new teacher." I wouldn't have to say that she had the bluest eyes in the world, or the prettiest brown-red hair. Gramps would see all that for himself.

But when I crawled out early for church on Sunday morning, we had ourselves a storm brewing like I'd never seen before. The wind was howling and the snow was drifting so bad you couldn't even see the barn.

"Whoo-ee," remarked Uncle Charlie as he looked out the frosted window, "would you look at her howl!"

"Guess this here winter is determined to make up for our fine fall," stated Grandpa.

"Gonna be tough gettin' to church," I mumbled, more to myself than to anyone else.

"Won't anyone be able to get to church this mornin'," Grandpa stated as known fact. "Doubt even the town folk will make it."

You can bet I was some disappointed about that. Suddenly the long, quiet Lord's Day stretched before me empty and desolate. How in the world would we ever fill it?

The only excitement in the day was fighting our way against the wind to care for the team, the cows, hogs and chickens. They were all mighty glad to see us. Back in the house, bone-chilled and tingling, we were all glad for a good wood supply against the cold.

After our dinner together, I helped Uncle Charlie with the dishes. We settled down with hot coffee and Aunt Lou's cookies to watch the storm and play checkers. Gramps took on Grandpa and Uncle Charlie challenged me. My mind wasn't on the game too much and I didn't play as well as I should have.

"I think I'll have a nap," stated Gramps, who often had a nap in the afternoon.

"Me, too," I said, standing up and yawning, and all eyes turned to look at me.

"Been studyin' too hard, Josh?" asked Grandpa.

"Well, no, not too hard," I stammered. "But I do need to study a fair bit to make up for all that time we lost."

I could tell all the menfolk approved of my statement.

Fact was, I *had* been studying hard. I guess I was out to prove to the new teacher that I had a "good mind," knowing he admired one and all. I wasn't sure how Camellia felt about a good mind, but I didn't think it would hurt my cause none to impress her father.

"Might as well have yer nap," Uncle Charlie said. "Nothin' better to do."

I did go to my room and lie down—but I couldn't sleep. I just lay there, tickling Pixie under the chin. I promised her we'd get back to town all right—before too long too.

I don't think Pixie was as interested in town as I was. I worried about Camellia and her folks maybe being caught short of wood or something and not making out well in the storm. I worried about other fellas maybe going over to check on how they were and making a good impression on her. I knew if I'd been in town, I sure would have been over there at her house, checking to see if there was anything I could do for them.

Thinking didn't help and sleep would not come. I pulled out one of my old storybooks from a trunk I had my "treasures" in and tried to read. Either the story had changed— or I had. I couldn't get interested in it—and it had been my favorite.

I finally gave up and just lay there listening to the wind howl. Would Aunt Lou and Uncle Nat be worried that we might try to come into town in the storm and then fret when we didn't arrive? No, they knew my grandpa better than that. He had far too much sense to head out into this storm.

When I heard voices down below, including Gramps, I knew all three men were around and stirring again. Then I heard the rattle of dishes—one of them was preparing our supper. I figured it must be chore time again, and I was glad for a good reason to leave my bed.

For two more days the wind howled and blew the snow

around. In some places the drifts were higher than my head. I didn't recall ever seeing a worse blizzard. We managed to keep ourselves quite busy, shoveling our way to the stock and chopping and hauling. Even so I chafed some.

On Wednesday the weather finally broke and the sun came out. But you could see it would be unwise to try to push a team through those drifts to town.

It turned out that I missed the whole week of school. I studied at home. It gave me something to do, and I sure didn't want to get behind the rest of my classmates.

On Sunday morning we did bundle up and head for church. Grandpa was worried about what Aunt Lou and Uncle Nat had been eating. They always got farm produce from us, like their milk and eggs and cream. Their extra garden vegetables and fruit were kept at the farm in the root cellar, too, and Grandpa always supplied them with fresh meat and poultry that was either just butchered or kept on big ice chunks in our sawdust-filled ice house.

"They do have 'em stores in town," Uncle Charlie reminded Grandpa.

"No reason to spend money when you don't need to," was Grandpa's response, so the sleigh was loaded with food, and we bundled up well and headed for church.

I put Pixie in her box in my bedroom when we got to Aunt Lou's and then helped unload the sleigh before we went to church. Uncle Nat was already over at the church, building up a good fire to take the chill off the cold room.

Aunt Lou said they had fared well during the storm, though Uncle Nat had fretted a bit about some of the parishioners, especially the older ones. He was afraid they might not have been prepared for the cold weather.

He had even brought Old Sam home with him and kept him on the living room couch, but Sam had left again some time during the night on Friday. Uncle Nat had supposed he had gone in search of a bottle.

Old Sam was the town drunk. I suppose there are nicer ways of stating it—but that's the plain fact.

He had been in our town for as long as I could remember.

I don't recall ever having heard a last name for him. Everyone just called him Sam, or Old Sam.

He had worked at odd jobs here and there when he had been a younger man and before the bottle took complete control of his life, but he didn't even try anymore. I don't know where he got money for booze. He sure never had money for food. Some of the town people gave him a meal now and then just out of charity. He didn't have money for clothes either. Uncle Nat watched that department and tried to keep Sam dressed so he wouldn't embarrass folk or freeze to death in the cold weather.

Truth was, Old Sam was as much a part of our town as the butcher or the grocer, and everyone sort of used him as the example of complete godlessness and waste. Mamas would say to their sons, "You don't want to turn out like Old Sam, do you?" The menfolk would say about their lazy employees that "he's about as useless as Old Sam," and angry fellas would say to one another, "Why don'tcha go join Old Sam, where ya belong?" or "You smell as bad as Old Sam"— but nobody could do anything to change Sam from what he was.

Uncle Nat had tried. Boy, had he tried. He was always trying to clean Sam up and feed him nourishing food. He tried even harder to get him to know that the only way he could *really* clean up his life and make something of himself was to give his life completely over to the Lord Jesus. I had heard Uncle Nat tell Sam that many times myself. But Sam would just whimper that it was too late. Nothing could be undone that was done. And then Uncle Nat would insist, "Jesus can do it, Sam. He can make a new man of you if you'll let Him. No sinner is too black for the Lord to wash clean as snow. No sin is too great for God to forgive," but Sam would just shake his head, clutch his bottle and whimper.

I knew, without even asking, that Uncle Nat had probably already been looking for Sam in all of his favorite hangouts— like the livery stable, the back porch of the grocer's, the shed in the schoolyard, and the little barn out back of the town hall. I knew, too, that as soon as the morning service was over, Uncle Nat would be out looking for Sam again.

When we entered the small church my eyes quickly scanned the room, but the Foggelson family was not in attendance. I was keenly disappointed. I sincerely hoped nothing had happened to any of them during the storm.

Avery and Willie came over to me and started talking about the blizzard here in town—the Smiths' chimney fire and the Bases running out of firewood and needing to burn some of the furniture, and how Mitch Turley froze the tip of his nose and needed to see the doc.

I wasn't too interested in all the news. I was still wondering about the Foggelsons.

It turned out that I really hadn't missed much school. It was Thursday before classes were held, and then only a few of the students braved the weather. More measles were going around. Folks hoped the cold weather would put a stop to the spread. Only one patient had been really sick—the little Williams girl. The doc was hoping she was now on the mend; but there was some concern about her eyesight, for some reason none of us really understood.

After the service we shared dinner at Aunt Lou's, and before we even had time for a visit Uncle Nat excused himself from the table. I knew he was off looking for Old Sam again. I pushed back, too, and went for my heavy coat.

"I'll help you," I said. "I'll take the road down past the school."

Uncle Nat nodded, appreciation in his eyes. We left the house together, while the three older men visited with Aunt Lou over coffee before helping her with the dinner dishes.

I hadn't bothered to explain to Uncle Nat that the Foggelsons lived down the school road. Here was a ready-made opportunity to check and be sure that everything was fine there.

When I got to the Foggelsons', I was relieved to see smoke curling briskly from both their chimneys. The house didn't look like it had suffered any from the storm, but I walked up to the back door and knocked anyway, practicing in my mind what I would say, depending on who answered. It was Mrs. Foggelson—at least I figured it must be her. She did look a lot like Camellia, with the same blue eyes and clear skin and hair almost as pretty, though she wore it all piled up on top of her head.

"Yes?" she said rather hesitantly.

"I'm Joshua Jones," I said quickly, to explain myself and keep her from shutting the door. "I'm one of your husband's students, and I just wanted to check to see that you're not needin' anything—I mean with the storm and all—I thought that—"

But she interrupted, "How sweet," sorta dragging out the words and smiling nice as she said them.

I stammered then. My planned speech went flying right out of my head and I couldn't think of one sensible thing to say.

"We are fine, Joshua," she was saying. "But we do thank you for stopping by. The storm was a nasty one, wasn't it?"

"I'm right glad," I stumbled, my face beginning to redden. "I mean, I'm glad you're fine."

"Would you like to come in?" she was asking, holding the door wide open for me.

Boy, would I have loved to have gone in, but I found myself saying, "Thank you, no, I've gotta get. I mean—I'm helpin' Uncle Nat look for Old Sam. I mean, well—he always worries that he might freeze to death—or somethin'." Then I hurried on, blurting out some further explanation that didn't need to be made, "He's not our kin or nothin'; it's just that Uncle Nat always worries over folks—I mean, he's the preacher and his job—" But I finally stopped, feeling more embarrassed than ever.

"I see," said the pretty Mrs. Foggelson, giving me another melting smile. I wasn't sure if she did see or not, but I knew I had to get out of there before I said something even dumber.

I mumbled a goodbye, placed my cap back on my cold head, and started off almost on the run.

It turned out I was the one to find Old Sam. He was huddled in a corner of the woodshed behind the town hotel. His teeth were chattering and his beard was matted, and even in the crisp cold winter air, he smelled bad. He was still clutching a bottle, though it was an empty one. I couldn't figure out why he wasn't dead. Guess maybe all the alcohol maybe preserved him, like cucumbers in vinegar, or something. I knew I couldn't move him all alone, and I didn't know what to do with him anyway, so I went home for help.

Uncle Nat was still out, so Uncle Charlie and Grandpa hitched the team and went off for Old Sam. When they got him back they put him to bed on a cot in the living room, and Aunt Lou made some hot soup to try to get down him. I left the rest of them fussing over him and went to my room. I figured I had already done my part. I wasn't too crazy over the dirty old coot anyway. But I knew Uncle Nat would be powerful glad to see he was still alive. I guess I was glad for that fact too.

Chapter 11

Camellia

Every fella in our school—every one in his right mind, that is—was sorta sweet on Camellia. As you can probably tell, I was no different. Some days I had so much trouble keeping my mind on my work that I scarce understood the words in my lesson books. This was new to me, having always being considered a good student and enjoying the work and all.

I managed somehow to keep up with the rest of the class, but I guess I picked up the new knowledge subconsciously or something, for I don't really remember learning it.

Every recess and noon hour we fellas spent our time trying to get Camellia's attention, though none of us would actually admit to it. Some were a little bolder than others. Me, I hung back trying not to look too forward, trying not to look too obvious, but all the time thinking of little things that I might do or say if I got the opportunity.

The opportunity came in rather a strange way.

For some reason I didn't understand, Camellia's pa seemed to take a liking to me. He talked with me a lot and often asked me to stay after classes just to chat about some book or some new idea. On several occasions he made a pleased comment about my "good mind."

Anyway I got the surprise of my life one day when Mr. Foggelson, Camellia's pa, asked me to stay after class again.

As I explained, staying after class was nothing new, the fellas were already teasing me some about that, but Mr. Foggelson's words sure did surprise me.

"Joshua," he said—he always called me Joshua, real proper-like—"Joshua, I wonder if you would have time to help me out."

I certainly wanted to help the Foggelson family if I could, but I wasn't sure about the time part. I did have a lot of chores to do at home, and I would need to check with Aunt Lou before I could give an answer. I figured Mr. Foggelson must have some wood that needed chopping or something like that, which could take a lot of time, all right.

Mr. Foggelson went on, "Camellia is having a bit of trouble with that new concept in geometry, and you have grasped it thoroughly. I thought she might find it easier to understand from one of her fellow students than she does when her father tries to explain it. I have a tendency to be a bit impatient with her at times, I fear. Do you think you could find the time?"

I would find the time. My head was nodding yes before I could even discover my voice.

"Very good," said Mr. Foggelson approvingly. "Would Wednesday after school suit you?"

I was nodding again and then my head began to clear, and I knew I'd better do some real thinking on the issue.

"I'll need to ask my aunt Lou," I managed. And then I even had the presence of mind to say, "Wednesday might not work. I have a lot of chorin' to do, and I need to get it all finished by prayer meetin' time."

"I see," said Mr. Foggelson rather slowly, a slight frown on his face.

"Oh, I'll do it," I hastened to inform him. "We'll arrange something, Aunt Lou and me—and I," I corrected myself quickly.

"Good," he said, his frown replaced by a somewhat distant smile.

"I'll check with her tonight and let you know in the morning, sir," I said, and with his nod of agreement I felt I was dismissed.

I left then as dignified as I could manage, careful not to put on my cap, or hoot, or run until I had left the schoolhouse steps.

I guess I ran all the way home, and when I got there I was so out of breath I couldn't even tell Aunt Lou my good news. I just sat there gulping air, my face flushed from the cold air and the run.

She laughed at me as she put the milk and cookies in front of me. She knew I had something exciting to share, and that I was near to busting for the want of telling it.

"Take your time, Josh," she said, patting my shoulder. "I'll be here when you catch your breath."

Pixie pushed against my leg, wanting up on my lap, and I scooped her up and shared a bit of my cookie. I thought Pixie would be interested in my news, too, but I couldn't tell her yet either.

Aunt Lou went to the back porch to get more wood for the fire. She seemed to take a little longer than usual, and I wondered if she was doing it on purpose to give me time to catch my breath.

When she came back, she started chatting right away— I think to give me even more time.

"I was just thinking, Josh, it is only three weeks till Christmas. Seems funny. I haven't even gotten in the Christmas mood yet, though we have been practicing the Christmas music for the church program. Still, it's coming soon, ready or not."

I nodded my head and washed down my mouthful of cookie with the cold milk.

"Anything special you want for Christmas, Josh?"

I hadn't been doing any thinking on that. I shook my head, trying at the same time to come up with an item so Aunt Lou would feel good about getting me something I "wanted."

I came up empty. Fact was I really had everything I needed. And Camellia's special friendship was about the only thing I was wanting, and I supposed Aunt Lou couldn't do much about getting that for me. I was rather on my own there.

I emptied the last of my milk and Aunt Lou pulled out a chair at the table and sat down.

"Can you talk now?" she asked, a bit of a twinkle in her eyes.

"Mr. Foggelson asked me for some help," I blurted out.

"Help?" Aunt Lou responded, curiosity in her face.

"With geometry."

"Help *him* in geometry?" teased Aunt Lou, but I knew she didn't need an answer to that.

"Sort of coachin'—or teachin'," I went on to explain.

"Oh—h," responded Aunt Lou, and she gave me one of her shining smiles as only Aunt Lou could when she was very pleased with me.

"You must be doing very well, Josh, for the teacher to pick you to tutor another student. I'm proud of you." And she reached out and placed her hand on my head for just a moment.

"Then I can do it?"

"Of course. I think it's an honor—and will also be a good experience for you."

"He suggested Wednesday night," I continued, "but I told him it takes all my time to get my chores done before prayer meetin'."

"Will another evening work?" Aunt Lou asked, genuinely concerned. "I mean," she went on, "if no other night works, I could help with the chores or—"

I stood up quickly, almost forgetting Pixie on my lap. I was shaking my head as I grabbed for Pixie.

"I'm sure we can work somethin' out for another time," I said, not wanting Aunt Lou to even consider choring when she had me around.

"Talk it over with your teacher," suggested Aunt Lou. "We certainly will co-operate in any way we can." I knew she and Uncle Nat would do their best to work it out so I could do the "tutoring."

I was turning to go get changed out of my school clothes when Aunt Lou's voice stopped me.

"Who's the lucky student, Josh?"

I turned, not understanding her for a moment.

"Who's the lucky student?" she asked again, "to have you for a tutor?"

Without me being able to stop it the red began to creep into my face. I wanted to turn away to hide my embarrassment but I knew that would be rude. I tried to keep my voice even, though the thumping of my heart was far from normal.

"Camellia," I stated as matter-of-factly as I could, trying hard to put no special emphasis on the name.

"Camellia?" said Aunt Lou.

"Camellia Foggelson," I stumbled on.

"Oh, the teacher's daughter. Then it *is* an honor, Joshua. If the teacher picked you to teach his own daughter, then he must have a high regard for you."

I stood there, still blushing, not knowing what to say and wishing to escape to the quietness and privacy of my own small bedroom.

"Is she a poor student?" queried my aunt.

"She's 'bout the best in the class," I blurted out too quickly. "She always leads everyone in English and Social Studies. She's real good at Art and Readin' and everything. She even beats me in Arithmetic an'—" I stopped. I realized I was sounding like I thought Aunt Lou had insulted her. I also realized Camellia was a good student. A very good student. She led the class in almost every subject. So why was I being asked to tutor her? I hadn't given it a thought before, I was so excited over the possibility of just being with her. And if I did take on tutoring her, could I keep my thoughts on the geometry problems long enough to be of any help to her? Some strange doubts and feelings began to flood over me. I turned to go to my room.

Aunt Lou must have sensed my confusion, for she did not question me further or try to stop me.

All the time I was changing into my clothes for chores, my mind wrestled with the problem. Why was Mr. Foggelson asking me to tutor his daughter who clearly needed no tutoring? Was *I* failing geometry? Was this a way to help me without me feeling embarrassed over it? No, that didn't make sense. I was having no trouble with the work. In fact, I had just gotten a grade of 98% on my last test. Was Camellia really having trouble with this part of the work? Well, maybe. Maybe she hadn't gotten her usual high-nineties score last time. I was sure Mr. Foggelson expected only top grades from her. Perhaps he really did want tutoring help for Camellia.

I tried to push the weighty problem to the back of my mind and think on other things, but it kept popping to the front again, insisting on my full attention.

I picked up Pixie and headed out through the kitchen to get my heavy coat.

"You'd best stay in," I told the little dog. "It's too cold out there for you tonight."

Aunt Lou, busy peeling the supper vegetables, gave me a smile as I walked by, but said nothing further about my tutoring. I was glad. I wasn't quite ready to discuss it yet. I had to do some more sorting out first. I had been so excited about it and was nearly bursting to share it with some of the fellas. Now I just wasn't so sure. Maybe I wouldn't say anything about it at all. Might be better if I sorta kept it to myself, at least until I had it figured out.

Chapter 12

The Tutoring

Mr. Foggelson's eyes met mine the next morning as soon as I entered the classroom. I could not avoid him without being rude, so I sorta smiled and nodded my head slightly, and he understood that I had talked to my aunt Lou and uncle Nat.

Fact was, we'd had quite a discussion about the matter. After the chores were all done, the evening meal over and we'd had our evening devotions together, Aunt Lou brought up the subject again.

"Josh has had quite an honor today," she told Uncle Nat. "The teacher has asked him to help his daughter, Camellia, with some geometry that she is not quite understanding."

Uncle Nat's eyes lifted from the Bible he was replacing on the small corner table.

"That so?" he said. "Good for you, Josh," and he gave me a smile and a playful slap on the back.

I blushed a bit and shifted my feet some.

"When?" asked Uncle Nat.

"We haven't worked that out yet," I stammered after Aunt Lou waited for me to answer the question. "He had suggested Wednesday, but I told him I couldn't get my chores done soon enough. It's all I can do to get finished in time for prayer meetin' and I sure wouldn't have time—"

"If it's the only night that will work for them, we probably could work something out," said Uncle Nat. "Maybe a bit more wood chopping other nights, and on Wednesday I could try to get home earlier and—"

"Ain't no sense you takin' on more," I found myself saying. I knew that Uncle Nat was already too busy. He hardly had any time at home.

"I'm sure another night will work just fine," I continued. "I'll talk to Mr. Foggelson tomorrow."

"We'll co-operate in any way that we can," said Uncle Nat as they both smiled at me, and I knew they would.

Then Uncle Nat turned very serious. He spoke slowly and deliberately, "This might be an answer to my prayers, Josh. I called on the Foggelsons as soon as they moved to town and invited them to join us in worship." Uncle Nat paused for a moment, and I knew he was carefully choosing each word. "Mr. Foggelson said they had no need nor interest in church. That it was for the deprived and unlearned—as a crutch— that educated men had other things than myths and fables to give their attention to. He also said his wife and daughter were free to make their own decision, but when his wife looked up after his comment, I got the feeling that the decision had already been made for her, too."

There was silence for several moments.

"Maybe God can use you in some way, Josh, to bring His light to this family."

The thought kinda scared me. I was no preacher or anything. If Uncle Nat had failed to convince the man, then surely there was nothing I could do. I mean, it was real scary—to have someone's eternal destiny, so to speak, resting on my shoulders. Actually, I expected to take that responsibility someday. I was sorta thinking about being a preacher like Uncle Nat. I really respected him—and so did the other people of the town. Wherever he went folks greeted him and doffed their caps and listened to what he had to say with real respect. And he was the one they called on when there was sickness or an accident or trouble of most any kind. I bet there wasn't a fella who got called on more—unless it was the doc. Even then the two of them most often ended up in the same house, for the same need—doc with his black medical bag and Uncle Nat with his black Book.

Well, even if I did hope to one day be a preacher too and looked up to by the people, I wasn't quite ready for that responsibility yet, and the thought of being the one to help some family, especially the family of my teacher, see the need for Christ and the church—well, I didn't know if I could do that. Still, I said nothing. Just squirmed a bit.

"Let's pray," suggested Uncle Nat.

We had just finished praying, but after a brief glimpse at Uncle Nat, then Aunt Lou, I bowed my head like they were doing.

"Dear Lord, our Father," began Uncle Nat. "We thank you for this opportunity that has come to Josh to enter the home of the Foggelsons. Help him to be sensitive to your leading and to let his light shine for you. May he be used of you, Lord, and be instrumental in bringing this family to the place where they realize that education, as good as it is, is not enough to prepare one for life after death. That one cannot better the mind sufficiently to redeem the soul—that only through the death and life of Jesus Christ can we have our sins forgiven and our lives changed. Amen."

I gave a great deal of thought to Uncle Nat's prayer. I had never considered the possibility of a man like Mr. Foggelson being denied heaven. I mean, he was decent, intelligent, and a gentleman. Everyone nodded to him and greeted him with respect. Yet here he was, not believing in God and not ready for heaven. If he should have an accident or a sickness and die—I didn't even want to think of it. It was easy for me to understand about Old Sam. He was wicked. The fella was always drunk. He couldn't even care for himself properly. He didn't wash, he didn't change his clothes. He didn't even eat most of the time. Uncle Nat had to look after him constantly and pour soup down him or he wouldn't even have survived from week to week. But Mr. Foggelson? It was awfully hard for me to put the two men in the same category—"lost."

So that's how I came to be back in class, trying not to let on to Mr. Foggelson that I knew he was a sinner, that he would not be allowed into heaven unless he chose to repent of his sin. It wasn't my rule, it was God's rule—it was that simple, that straightforward. There was no middle road. No other option. There was only heaven and hell, and heaven was for those who called on the Lord God to forgive them for their wrongdoings. If one chose to ignore God or deny that He had a right to direct one's life, that person would not be allowed into heaven, no matter how good other people thought he was.

I was glad we went right to our history lesson so I could lower my eyes to my book.

At recess and lunch time I didn't say anything to the other fellas about tutoring Camellia. Not even to Willie or Avery. I tried to join in with the games as usual, but it was difficult. My mind just wasn't on them. I think the others noticed my lack of concentration and my quietness—I caught a few glances my way, but no one said anything, for which I was glad.

I also noticed a few glances from Camellia. She looked over my way several times and once even smiled before I could turn away. My stomach gave a flop and I missed the tag on Avery. I tried to fake a trip so the fellas wouldn't guess what had really happened. I don't think I brought it off very well.

After school I knew I would be questioned by Mr. Foggelson, so I didn't even try to hurry putting away my books and gathering up my lessons to take home.

He came with a big smile.

"Well, Joshua, did you get permission from your aunt and uncle?"

"Yes, sir," I answered, swallowing hard and trying to raise my eyes to Mr. Foggelson's face.

"Good," he beamed. "When can you begin?"

"Thursdays seem to be best, sir. Right after school, if that suits you."

"That suits me just fine. And Camellia, too. She's happy to hear you can help her."

I blushed, hating myself for doing so.

This was Wednesday and I had to get right home to do the chores. I was glad for an excuse to get away quickly.

I gathered my books and nodded at Mr. Foggelson.

"I'll plan on tomorrow then. Right after school."

"Fine," he said and reached out and placed a hand on my shoulder. It was the first time he had touched me, the first I had seen him touch any of the students. Not even Camellia, though I was sure that in the privacy of their own home there must be father-daughter contact. I felt a bit embarrassed, though I did not know why. I was used to a great deal of touching. Why, in my family we were always hugging and slapping one another on the back and patting on the head and squeezing the hand and all sorts of nice family things.

Still, it wasn't like your teacher laying his hand on your shoulder, like you were someone special to him—and you weren't just sure what the "special" was. I didn't know what to say or do, so I just cleared my throat and looked down at my books again.

"I'll see you tomorrow," I said awkwardly and headed for the door.

I both dreaded and anticipated the day for the first tutoring and, boy, can that ever mix you up inside!

I did have the sense to set aside my geometry book after class the next day. I fumbled around at my desk, pushing books around, sorting and resorting until I was sure the fellas had left the room.

I finally dared to look up, half expecting Mr. Foggelson to be standing at my desk with instructions on how I was to teach his daughter. But it was Camellia's deep blue eyes that met mine. She gave me a wonderful smile, and I nearly dropped the geometry book I held in my hand. I looked down again, fumbled some more with my book and nearly choked mid-swallow.

"Are you ready?" she asked nicely and I nodded, then let my eyes wander to the boards that Mr. Foggelson was meticulously cleaning.

"Papa will be home later," she said in answer to my unasked question. "He always stays to clean the chalkboards and put some lessons on for the next day."

I nodded again, but I felt like I was rooted to my spot.

"Let's go then," she offered. "Papa said you have lots of chores after school so I mustn't waste your time."

I forced my wooden legs to move and followed her out of the schoolroom. We were halfway across the yard before I realized she was carrying a load of books. I mumbled some kind of apology and reached to take them from her.

"Thank you, Joshua," she said with just a hint of appealing shyness, dropping her long, dark eyelashes. It rather threw me. I had never had a girl flirt with me before. At least not one like Camellia.

When we got to her house her mother greeted us warmly and waved us toward the tea and fancy pastries placed on the table. I was not a tea drinker. I didn't care much for the stuff and I had always been encouraged to drink milk, a growing boy needing lots of it to make his teeth and bones strong and all, but I would have died before I would have admitted that to Camellia or her ma.

"Do you care for cream or sugar?" asked Camellia courteously, about to pour.

I tried to remember what Aunt Lou or Grandpa took in their teas but my mind went blank. "No, thank you," I finally mumbled. "Just bare."

Camellia's eyelashes fluttered softly as she glanced at me, and I knew I had said something dumb. What was it that one said about tea anyway? I knew Gramps always had his coffee "black," but tea wasn't black. What was it, anyway?

"I like a little cream in mine," Camellia was saying. "Papa's always teasing me, saying it will make me fat someday, but I use it anyway." She laughed merrily.

I couldn't imagine her fat but didn't know if I should say so.

She passed me a pastry then. It looked about the size of one mouthful, but I knew better than to take two. Besides, I wasn't sure just what the thing was and how one went about eating it. I laid mine down on the small flowery plate that sat on the white tablecloth and waited for Camellia to lead the way.

She picked hers up nimbly in her fingers and took a dainty nibble. I followed suit. Only for some reason mine didn't work quite like hers had. I don't know if I had gotten a faulty one or what, but just as I went to take a teeny bite from the side like Camellia had done, the fool thing crumbled in my fingers and fell all over the tablecloth, leaving me with empty air and a red face.

I felt like a dolt, that's how I felt, but Camellia pretended not to mind.

"I've always told Mama that those dainty little pastries were not made to be held in the strong hands of a man," she said. "Their fingers are just too used to a firm grip on things." And so saying she leaned right over toward me, swept the crumbs into her own plate and took them away from the table. When she returned she brought with her a small fork with a short handle, and she passed me another pastry.

"They are difficult to eat with a fork, too," she whispered confidentially, "but it might be a little easier."

I somehow managed to get most of that pastry to my lips. By the time I was finished I was glad the thing hadn't been any bigger. I was almost sweating with the effort—and I still had that cup of tea ahead of me.

The teacup with its little handle was not much easier to manage than the pastry had been. It must have been designed for a creature with only one finger and a thumb. I didn't know what to do with the other three—no matter how I held the cup they all got in the way.

Camellia tried to put me at ease and I appreciated her effort. *Not only pretty, she is sensitive and caring, too,* I thought, and that made me like her even more.

"We will study in the sitting room," she informed me when we had finally freed ourselves of the tea and dainties, and with great relief I followed her away from that table with its linen cloth and china cups.

The sitting room was comfortably furnished, and we chose a settee by the large window and spread our books out on the small table before it. Somehow I had the feeling that the table had been placed there purposely for our use.

"What part you wishin' to study?" I began, opening my text.

"None of it," she responded. I'm sure I couldn't have looked as astounded as I felt, but she giggled, softly and bubbly, like our little crik when it splashes over pebbles on a sandbar.

Now, I had never cared much for girls giggling, but Camellia's was different. It made me feel like giggling, too, and I had to check myself before some dumb sound came out of my mouth. Instead, I just smiled, a blush making my cheeks hot. I knew there was a secret joke here, but I wasn't sure just what it was.

"One is supposed to be honest, isn't one?" Camellia was saying pertly, her blue eyes twinkling with merriment.

I nodded. Certainly one was to be honest.

"Well, I'm honest. I wish we didn't need to study."

"I'm sorry," I began. "I didn't know that your pa was *makin'* you—"

But I got no further.

"Oh, Joshua," she stopped me, reaching out one soft hand to lay gently on mine. "This wasn't Papa's idea."

I was totally lost. If it wasn't her pa's idea that we study and she didn't wish to study, then what was I doing in her house?

"I coaxed Papa to ask you," she said frankly in response to my perplexed look.

"You did?" I stammered.

"Yes," she said with a flip of her coppery curls. "I did."

"But why?"

"Why?" She seemed a little annoyed at my question.

"Why—if you don't want to study—?"

She looked at me like I was a child. But then she tossed her hair again and fluttered those long eyelashes.

"I just wanted to get to know you better—to talk."

I was dumbfounded. I stared at her, my mouth open and my heart pounding wildly. I wanted to ask "why?" again but

I didn't dare. Camellia would expect me to know the answer, and I didn't—not yet at least. It might take a good deal of sorting out.

I swallowed hard and turned back to the book, thumbing through the pages.

"Well—well—" I began, "guess we can talk and study, too."

She rewarded me with a flashing smile and slid over so we could both share my geometry text. Hers lay on the table, unopened.

We started through the text page by page, and I found there was little if any help needed by Camellia. She understood the concepts most as good as I did.

It was nearly time for me to be hurrying off home when she looked up from the text. "Do you have any brothers or sisters, Joshua?" she surprised me by asking.

I shook my head.

"Me neither." There was silence for a minute. I guess we were both thinking some on that.

"Does it make you angry?" she asked in a quiet voice.

"Angry?" Though I missed having a brother or a sister, I had never thought of being angry about it.

"Yes. Angry."

"Guess not. Why?"

Her brow furrowed in deep thought or consternation, I wasn't sure which. "Sometimes it makes me angry," she confided. "It used to make me terribly angry. I didn't think it was fair at all. Everyone should have more family than just a mother and a father. Don't you think?"

I shrugged my shoulders carelessly. I wasn't sure I was ready to tell Camellia the fact that I didn't even have that much family.

"But I don't get as angry anymore," went on Camellia. "In fact, I guess there are some good things about being an only child."

"Like?" I asked.

"Well—" she said slowly. "Like you."

"Me?"

"Sure. If I was not an only child, then I probably wouldn't get my own way all the time, and Mama and Papa might not have agreed to let you tutor me."

I felt my mouth drop open again.

"It wasn't hard to convince Papa. He gives me anything I want," said Camellia, "but Mama can be awfully stubborn sometimes."

I had never heard a person talk like that about their own parents before, and I must confess I was a bit shocked. But Camellia said it so innocently, so frankly, that I found myself excusing her.

"Do you always get your own way, Joshua?" she asked me.

"I—I don't know," I said truthfully. "I've never thought on it before. I guess I'd never thought to even try."

"You haven't?" The idea seemed preposterous to her.

"Well—ah—well, they let me have my dog, Pixie, an'—"

"You have a dog?"

I nodded.

"Oh, you're so lucky. I've always wanted a dog, but Mama says, 'Positively not.' She has allergies. And she is so—so—"

"Stubborn," I whispered, and we both burst into laughter.

The laughing must have jerked me back to reality, for my eyes traveled to the clock on the mantel.

"I've got to get," I said, jumping to my feet. "I'll never get my chores done if I don't hurry."

She looked like she wanted to ask me to stay longer, but she bit her lip and didn't say anything.

"Thank you, Joshua, for your help," she said instead. "I'll see you next Thursday."

Her comment brought me up short. I hardly knew what to say or how to say it.

"Camellia," I began, "you know the geometry as good as I do. I really didn't help you none."

"But you did!" she insisted. "Please, Joshua. You promised. Please say you'll come again."

That part was right, I had promised. The whole thing didn't make much sense. It wasn't that I didn't want to come.

And maybe—maybe I had helped her some.

I smiled.

"Sure," I agreed. "I promised. I'll see you next Thursday."

"Joshua," she said with a big smile, "could you show me your little dog sometime?"

"I'd love to. She can do all kinds of tricks and everything."

"But you can't bring her here," she frowned, "on account of Mama's allergies."

"Then you can come home with me and see her. Ask your folks. Aunt Lou would love to meet you."

She smiled again—and I took that smile all the way home with me.

Chapter 13

Good Old-Fashioned School Days?

When I got to school the next morning, the word had already gotten around that I had been seen carrying Camellia's books home. I never did find out who saw me and passed the news along, but it seemed to have done a bit of growing with its travels.

Avery met me by the path that leads up to the school, just below the bare, gnarled branches of the old maple tree the town fathers had planted there so many years before our time.

His first words were, "Is it true?"

"Is what true?" I responded innocently.

" 'Bout you and Camellia?"

My face started to redden. I had no idea what Avery had heard, but I had me a sinking feeling that some of it might be based on facts.

"I dunno," I said slowly, moving past Avery to continue up the path. "What've ya heard?"

"That you went home with Camellia."

I nodded, agreeing that I had. "Her pa asked me to help her some with her geometry." That sounded reasonable enough to me, but it didn't to Avery.

"Camellia?" he snorted. "Camellia? Camellia don't need help with nothin'."

Just then Willie and Jack sauntered up.

"Hey, listen to this, fellas," Avery called out before they even joined us. "Josh here went home with Camellia to *help* her with her *geometry*." He emphasized the words "help" and "geometry," and just as he had expected, the other two fellas stopped short and howled.

"Camellia?"

"Help with geometry?"

"Very funny, Josh!"

"Honest!" I argued as I was slapped on the back and punched on the arm, my face getting redder by the minute. "Her pa asked me to."

"Oh, come on, Josh," said Jack scornfully. "We're not dumb enough to believe that story."

"What really happened?" demanded Avery.

But before I could even answer, Jack was continuing. "I s'pose that's why you carried her books and held her hand, too."

"I did not," I denied hotly.

"An' I s'pose that's why you stayed at her house till almost dark," went on Tom Foster, who had just joined the inquisition.

"An' here you were pretendin' to not even be interested in her," went on Jack. "Whenever we'd talk about her or somethin', you'd hush us up, or move away from us, or change the subject or somethin'. 'We shouldn't talk about people behind their back,' you said. All you really wanted was to have her all to yourself." Jack's tone was so sarcastic, all I could do was stare at him.

But Willie was laughing. He was in the mood for doing a little teasing.

"An' I s'pose you had 'tea' with her mother," he said, and he held his fingers in a ridiculous pose and pretended to sip from a dainty cup.

"I did not," I denied, and then remembered the small cups and the flimsy pastries. Well, it hadn't been with her mother.

"An' her pa said, 'Josh-u-a, my boy, are your in-ten-tions

hon-or-able?' " went on Tom, exaggerating every word and mannerism.

He somehow managed to catch the look of Mr. Foggelson and I suppose even I would have laughed had not the joke been on me. Willie and Avery howled. Then I noticed that Jack didn't join the laughter. His face looked about as red as mine felt. It took me a moment to realize why.

Jack was sore. I knew he had been making quite a fuss over Camellia, but I sure hadn't expected him to carry on in this fashion.

My face was getting redder too, a lot of it from the anger churning away on my insides. I didn't know where to start with my denying; so much of what was being said was the truth that it was hard to sort it out from the errors. I knew then why Gramps had tried to explain to me how dangerous half-truths are. A downright lie you can dismiss in a hurry, but when it gets all tangled up with a smattering of truth, it is awfully hard to untangle.

I was genuinely saved by the bell. I had never been so glad to hear it ring in all my life.

We ran toward the schoolhouse, but even as we tore over the schoolhouse yard, I was aware of Jack's angry glances my way. When we jostled our way out of the boys' cloakroom and Camellia was just leaving the girls', her bright hair tossing about her shoulders and her cheeks flushed pink from the chill morning air, Jack gave me another black look. And then, to make matters even worse, Camellia flashed me one of her dazzling smiles and said, "Good morning, Joshua," very softly, but it wasn't soft enough for the other boys not to hear.

Willie and Avery were fit to be tied. They jabbed me with their elbows and sniggered behind their wind-cold hands. Tom stuck out his foot to trip me and almost succeeded. But it was Jack that bothered me the most. He glared at me like I was suddenly his worst enemy. My face flushed red and my head clouded with confusion. What was all of this about anyway?

The day didn't improve much. The boys teased me every

chance they got. Camellia flashed little smiles and fluttered her long eyelashes. Her silent signals made shivery feelings go slithering up my spine, but I hoped with all my heart that no one else was catching her at it.

By noon it was not only the boys but the girls as well who were teasing me. They weren't as bold about it, but the glances, the giggles, the laughter, all made me most uncomfortable. I was beginning to wish I had never seen or heard of Camellia Foggelson.

But, no, that wasn't fair—nor true. I knew that deep inside me, every time I stole a brief look at Camellia.

Near the end of the class, Mr. Foggelson caught my eye and gave me a bit of a nod, which I had come to recognize as his signal that he wanted me to remain behind after class. Of all days to be doing that! The fellas would really make a case of it.

At last the room seemed to be empty. I was still shuffling books around and pretending to look for something I couldn't find. Mr. Foggelson moved from the chalkboards back toward my desk. I knew I had to look up. But, boy, it was hard to raise my eyes.

"How's the tutoring going, Josh-u-a?"

He really did say my name that way. I hadn't noticed it before.

"Fine, sir," I responded as clearly as my dry mouth would allow me.

He nodded. "Camellia seems to understand the concept much better now."

I let the words settle about us, wondering just what to say next. We were both silent. It seemed like hours.

"Then she won't need any more help?" I asked, wondering if that made me sorrowful or relieved.

"Oh yes," he cut in quickly. "I'm sure she would appreciate a little more of your time—if you can spare it."

I wondered if he could hear my heart pounding, and then blushed at the thoughts of my classmates' taunts. I swallowed again, then slowly nodded my assent.

Mr. Foggelson sat down on the desk in front of me, a place

we students were forbidden to sit. Slowly he brushed the chalk dust from his fingers. Then he pulled a white handkerchief from his pocket and wiped his hands clean. He had a strange look on his face—like disdain or disgust or something.

"Fool dust," he muttered. "Gets on everything. Your hands, your clothes—even up your nose."

I didn't know how to respond so I didn't say anything.

"Don't ever be a teacher, Joshua," he said, still pronouncing my name like each syllable stood alone. He surprised me with the intensity in his voice as he stared over my head at some spot in the back of the room. "Poor pay, long hours, and a tough job. Day after day trying to pound a few facts into dense, uncaring little heads."

I wondered if he remembered I was still in the room. He seemed to be talking to himself—and he sounded bitter and depressed.

I still did not make any comment.

Suddenly he swung back to me, carefully tucking the handkerchief back into his trouser pocket. His expression changed and his eyes looked alive again.

"You have a good mind, Joshua. The best I've ever had the privilege of working with. I can see your face light up with understanding and appreciation. You can go far, Joshua. Be anything you want to be."

I knew that somehow my ability to learn had brought some strange joy to Mr. Foggelson. I couldn't understand just why, but it was enough to know that I had pleased him. I knew he was paying me a high compliment, yet I didn't know what to say in response.

"How would *you* feel about some special tutoring, Joshua?"

I licked my lips and swallowed again. I wasn't sure just what he meant by his question. Was he proposing now that *Camellia* tutor *me*? Boy, that would really make me the laughingstock of the school.

"I have a good library of sorts, Joshua. Oh, it's not big or grand, but it has some good basic books—books that would provide you with a great deal of information. I would no more consider bringing my books into the classroom for all of the students to paw over and mutilate and soil than—than throwing my daughter to the lions. But I would be happy to allow you the privilege of studying them—in my home—and of discussing the contents with me if you desire. What do you think?"

I'm sure my mouth, as usual these days, hung open. I didn't know what to think. I did love books, I did love learning new things—but Mr. Foggelson's private collection? Would I be careful enough? Would I understand them? Would I find the time? It all made my head spin. And what about the fellas? If I spent even more time at the Foggelsons', it was bound to mean more jokes.

I knew Mr. Foggelson was waiting for my answer, but I still wasn't sure what it should be.

I swallowed nervously and forced myself to begin, even though I still wasn't sure what words my voice would form.

"That's very kind, sir. I'm much obliged. I don't really know what to say. I mean—well, I—I . . ."

I stammered to a halt and Mr. Foggelson took over.

"You do enjoy books?"

"Oh yes, sir." That was not hard to answer.

"Then why the hesitation?"

"Well, I—I," I stumbled on, "I never thought of having so many books at one time—to learn from—an' these are your own special books. I'd hate to mess 'em up or anything."

"I wouldn't be afraid of you soiling my books, Joshua," said the teacher. "I know you will give them your full respect."

"Yes, sir," I hurriedly assured him.

"Well—?"

"I'll need to check at home. I mean—I have . . ." I fumbled for words again.

"Your chores. I know. But I'm sure we can work out something. Perhaps you would have some free time on Sunday afternoons."

I must have blinked. Studying was not done on Sundays

at our house—not even studying for enjoyment.

"Not on the Lord's Day, sir," I blurted out before I could even think about my selection of words.

Mr. Foggelson's eyes darkened. "I see," he said, but I wondered if he really did.

"Saturday?"

"I always go home to the farm after school on Friday night or else early Saturday mornin'. Grandpa comes for me. I stay all day Saturday and most of Sunday with the menfolk."

"And chores every night?" questioned Mr. Foggelson.

I nodded.

Mr. Foggelson stood up, still brushing imaginary chalk dust from his hands.

"So we have a problem?"

"I'll ask," I cut in quickly. "I'll talk to Aunt Lou—it's gonna be hard to work it in. But I'll ask."

"It's not that I want to be pushy, Joshua. It's just that in my years of teaching I have never found a mind like yours. It would be—it would be a shame to waste it. Both for your sake—and for mine."

I didn't know exactly what Mr. Foggelson was trying to say, but I nodded anyway. I did appreciate the fact that he was going out of his way to be kind to me and to encourage me to use the mind that God had given me. I smiled my thanks and began to gather up my books, but Mr. Foggelson was not done yet.

"Have you given consideration to what you'd like to do with your life, Joshua? A lawyer? A surgeon? An architect?"

I hadn't given much thought to any of those things. But I had thought about what I might like to do with my life, all right.

I smiled confidently at my teacher as I answered, "Yes, sir. A minister."

"A minister?" Mr. Foggelson shook his head slightly as if to clear cobwebs. I thought perhaps he had not understood me.

"A minister—like my uncle Nat," I explained to him.

"Nat? Oh, yes. Nathaniel Crawford is your uncle, isn't he? I had forgotten."

"Yep," I said with a great deal of pride, "he's my uncle."

I guess I had expected Mr. Foggelson to greet my announcement with a great deal of enthusiasm. He didn't. He didn't seem pleased at all. I couldn't understand it. But then, I remembered, Mr. Foggelson did not attend church. He most likely did not understand much about being a pastor. Maybe I could bring a few of Uncle Nat's precious books with me when I came to read from Mr. Foggelson's library.

I looked up. Mr. Foggelson was clearing his throat. Then he said a very unusual thing—more to himself than to me. "We'll see," he said. "We'll wait and see."

Chapter 14

Revenge

I was still getting a great deal of ribbing at school. The fellas got a lot of laughs from it but they meant no harm. It wasn't that way with Jack Berry. He had been my friend, a close friend. Now he rarely even spoke to me, just about me—and everything he had to say was mean and cutting.

I was really sorry about this. I didn't like having an enemy. I'd never had one before. Was he sore, too, about not getting to go on the camping trip? I just didn't know what to do.

I knew what the Bible said about enemies—that we are to love them, to do good to them. But, boy, it sure was hard to be nice to Jack Berry. He seemed to spend his nights thinking up mean things to say about me, and his days saying them.

I tried to ignore the insults but it sure got tough. Even the other fellas were beginning to get on me about the situation. They said I shouldn't allow Jack to say those things, that I should stand up to him. I tried to shrug it off.

Willie was the only one who really understood how I was feeling.

"It's tough, Josh," he said. "Doing what you know Jesus would do is really tough sometimes."

"Turning the other cheek" was what Willie said the Bible called it. Though he acknowledged that not defending myself

was tough, that was exactly what Willie expected a follower
of Jesus to do.

Then one Thursday everything all broke loose.

I had gone again to Camellia's house and, after our tea
and pastries—which I still didn't manage too well—we spent
some time studying. I would have stuck with it longer, but
after a few minutes of working over the geometry text, Camellia started talking about other things.

She was bright, lively, exciting, and it was fun talking to
her. It was easy for me to just let the book slide to the table
and listen to the music of her voice. When I finally pulled
myself away, gathered up my books and my coat and left her
house, I was in a big hurry. I was later than I should have
been and I had chores waiting for me at home.

I was just running by the darkened schoolyard, my breath
puffing out ahead of me in cloudy little spurts of frost, when
I heard an unexpected shuffling sound. Before I could even
turn to look, someone grabbed me and a fist whirled through
the air and hit me right in the face.

I hollered out with surprise and fright and my book went
flying through the air and landed somewhere in the dark
bushes just beyond me.

The fist hit me again, and this time pain streaked through
my right eye. It made tears stream down my face so I couldn't
even see my assailant.

I had never fought before in my life, but suddenly I was
fighting as if my very life depended upon it—for all I knew,
maybe it did.

As we traded punch for punch, I could tell whoever had
jumped me was about my size and weight. I still couldn't see,
so I had to cling to him with one hand and swing with the
other. Most of my punches missed, but a few of them were
solid hits. The other fella responded in grunts or cries of pain
that made me fight even harder.

It was hard and slippery under foot because of the frozen
ground, and as we tussled and pulled at one another, swinging whenever we could get a hand free, our breathing became
more and more labored. Once or twice I heard a tearing sound

but I didn't know, nor care, whose clothes were being ripped in the exchange. I was far too busy trying to save myself from who knew what.

I stopped worrying about who I was fighting and why, just kept on swinging as hard and effectively as I could. And then a solid blow caught me right on the chin, and I felt my knees turn to mush.

I didn't realize it at the time, but it would be several weeks until I was able to remember and sort out exactly what happened after that. Reconstructing events later, I recalled I had tried to stay on my feet, but the slippery ground and our tangled legs didn't help my sense of balance any, and I felt myself slowly going down.

"That oughta teach ya!" a familiar voice ground out between gasps for air, and I knew that it was Jack Berry who had attacked me.

A fiery anger went all through me like a knife blade. I tried to force my weak legs to work so they would hold me up long enough for another punch. But I couldn't stay on my feet. My head hit something solid and everything went black.

When I came to, I forced my eyes open, wondering where I was and what had happened to me. Darkness had totally taken over our small town. I did not know how long since I had left the Foggelsons. I did know that I hurt. My knuckles hurt, my face hurt, and my head hurt worst of all.

Realization flooded over me as I lifted my hand to my face. Even that movement made pain shoot all through me. I could feel a damp, sticky substance wetting my fingers. I felt a cut above my eye and knew my nose had been bleeding. Beyond that I didn't think I was hurt too bad except for my pounding head. If only I could get my legs under me again. But they just wouldn't co-operate.

I could feel the chill of the frozen earth beneath me seeping through my school jacket, and I found myself shivering with cold and wishing for my good, old, warm chore coat.

I should be home, I'm late for my chores. Aunt Lou will be worrying, were my fuzzy thoughts.

I was still laying there, trying to get my frozen fingers to button my jacket when I heard shuffling feet again. I gathered all my strength in one more effort to get to my feet. Then I heard the unmistakable mutterings of Old Sam. I could tell he was drunk as usual. And then there was a loud hiccup and Old Sam was stumbling over me to end up on the frozen ground.

He said a few mumbled unrepeatable words, and struggled to get to his feet. His legs didn't seem to work much better than mine, and he sprawled out on top of me again, banging my aching face with one boney elbow.

"Ohh," I groaned. "Watch it, Sam, will ya?"

"Joshsh?" questioned Sam in the darkness. "Joshsh?" he muttered again. Another hiccup followed. "Joshsh, that you?"

"Yeah, it's me."

I tried to roll Sam off so I could get to my feet. I couldn't do either. He made no attempt to help me. Just lay there like a limp sack.

"Sam," I implored helplessly, a hint of anger in my voice, "get up, will ya? At least get off me."

With a loud "hick" Sam rolled off me, mumbling to himself as he did so. Sam's mumbling was sort of a town joke. We fellas had never been able to figure out if he was trying to talk or sing.

Then he was on his knees fumbling around in the darkness, and I knew he must have lost his precious bottle.

I finally managed to get myself to a sitting position. My head was throbbing and spinning. I still couldn't pull myself to my feet. In fact, I wasn't too sure where my feet were.

Old Sam, still searching for his beloved bottle, muttered something about a "dumb book," and something clicked in my mind.

"That's my book," I said quickly, afraid Old Sam would throw it away.

He shoved my book toward me and went on feeling around on his hands and knees. He must have found what he was looking for, for he sighed and mumbled in his funny singsongy voice, and then I heard him swigging from his bottle again.

He probably emptied it because he turned his attention back to me.

"Ya hurt, Joshsh?"

I thought that was quite apparent, but for someone like Sam who spent a good deal of his time on the ground, perhaps it was a reasonable question.

"Yeah," I said, trying to keep the moan from my voice. "Yeah, I'm hurt."

"What'sh happened?"

"Guess—guess I hit my head."

I hoped Sam would ask no more questions.

"I'll help ya home."

It made me want to laugh. In his present state, Sam probably didn't even know which direction my home was.

"Just help me up," I told him. "I'll make it home."

That statement was a bit presumptuous. Even with Old Sam's help I had a hard time getting to my feet, much less putting one foot in front of the other. Of course his wasn't the steadiest help ever offered. Our first try landed us both back on the ground. But you had to give Old Sam credit for persistence. He kept right on tugging and pulling until somehow we were both on our feet again. I wasn't sure who was holding up who.

I found my book and tucked it under my coat and we started off, our arms around one another in some strange way. Shuffling our feet along, we felt our way down the street. The only light to guide us was the anemic splashes from small windows in the town dwellings.

My body was shaking with cold and shock. Sam did not seem to notice the cold, though the coat Uncle Nat had provided for him was not much warmer than my own.

We stumbled along together, me confused and aching, and Sam likely wondering where he could find another bottle.

Then I realized it was snowing. Large, flowery flakes drifted down to cover our head and shoulders. Even in my present state I enjoyed the snow.

"Almost home," Old Sam was muttering—and, squinting through the flurries, I could see that we were. Somehow, even in his drunken condition, he had found the way.

I still remember the flood of yellow lamplight and the rush of warm air when Old Sam pounded on the door with one foot and it opened to us. I remember hearing Aunt Lou's little cry of "Josh!" But that is all I can recall.

The next thing I knew Doc was bending over me and I was safely tucked in my own bed, with Aunt Lou and Uncle Nat hovering nearby.

From the parlor came the snoring sounds I had heard many times before, and I knew Old Sam had been "souped" and "bedded" and would be spending at least this night sheltered from the winter's cold.

Chapter 15

Questions and Answers

I awoke the next morning with a bad headache. My mouth felt dry and sore and one eye was swollen shut.

Aunt Lou was stirring about my room and the lamp was still lit on the bedside table. At the time, I couldn't even think properly to wonder if she had been there all night.

She moved close to my bed and bent over me. From the next room came the familiar sounds of snoring and someone else, likely Uncle Nat, tending the fire.

"How're you feeling?" Aunt Lou asked softly as though the sound of her voice might make me suffer even more.

I tried to shake my head because I didn't feel like I would be able to talk, but it hurt too much to move.

"Can I get you anything?" asked Aunt Lou, and I somehow got the message to her that I would like a drink.

"Just a sip," she told me. "Doc says you have a concussion and shouldn't put much in your stomach in case it won't stay down."

I sipped. The water had barely touched my parched lips when Aunt Lou withdrew the cup. I wanted to protest but the right sounds didn't come.

"Doc said that you'll be just fine in a day or two," Aunt Lou was assuring me.

I tried to nod in agreement, but stopped myself.

"Nat rode out to the farm last night to let them know,"

Aunt Lou told me. "They wanted to come right in, but Nat convinced them that Doc was taking good care of you and that it would be fine for them to wait until this morning."

"What day is it?" I managed to ask through swollen lips.

"Don't you remember? This is Friday."

Friday. Then I should be in school. In the afternoon Grandpa would be coming for me. I wasn't sure if I would be quite ready to go.

"Nat will stop by the school and tell your teacher that you won't be in class today," Aunt Lou was continuing. "We hope that by Monday you'll be just fine again."

Did she mean I would not be going to the farm? That I would spend the entire weekend confined to my bed?

"What happened?" I mumbled.

"We were hoping you'd be able to tell us that," said Aunt Lou. "Don't you remember anything about it?"

I tried to shake the fog from my brain.

Nothing was clear and I didn't want to try to think. My head hurt me enough with just the effort of laying it on my pillow.

"Doc left you another pill," Aunt Lou said. "Let me help you," and she placed the pill between my swollen lips and lifted my head slightly so I could swallow it with a sip of water.

I slept again then. When I awoke my head ached a little less. Gramps was sitting in my room holding a book on his lap and looking out the window at the snow gently sifting down.

I stirred so I could see the snow better and with the movement came sharp pain. I groaned and Gramps was immediately beside my bed.

"You okay, Joshua?" he asked me, his eyes filled with concern.

I gave my head a moment to settle down again.

"Yeah," I mumbled. I tried to lick my lips but that stung even more.

"Have a sip of water," Gramps offered and he held the cup to my mouth just a second longer than Aunt Lou had.

From the kitchen I could hear the sound of quiet voices, and I knew the rest of the family were gathered waiting for me to return to wakefulness.

"You've been sleeping for some time, Joshua," Gramps was saying. "Are you feeling any better?"

I wasn't sure. My head still hurt pretty bad but it was tolerable if I held it still.

"It's almost time for another tablet," Gramps went on.

"It's snowin'," I murmured. "How much?"

Gramps smiled. I think that simple question was a great relief to him.

"We've had about three inches already, Joshua, and it looks like we're going to get lots more."

"Good," I said. "We can have Christmas."

The earlier snow was already rutted, splashed with the dirty stains of shuffling feet and wagon wheels. I had never felt that such snow was fit for Christmas, even though I realized a messy ground would not keep Christmas from coming. But for me a "real" Christmas, Christmas the way it should be, meant white freshness covering our world.

I guess Gramps understood, for he grinned widely.

"We sure can, Joshua," he said. "We sure can."

My door opened a crack and Grandpa peeked around it. He probably had done the same thing many times over the last hour. At Gramps' nod the door opened farther and Grandpa came in.

He stood looking down at me for a long time, his throat working and his gray mustache twitching slightly. His eyes were shiny with wetness.

"How are you, Boy?" he finally asked.

"Okay," I managed as he reached out a calloused hand and laid it gently on my forehead.

There was a flash of movement through the door and Pixie bounded up on my bed.

"Forgot to shut that door," Grandpa muttered in apology, moving to lift Pixie down from my bed.

"She's okay," I quickly informed him and reached out a hand to fluff the silky fur on her head. Even that movement hurt and I scrunched my eyes tightly against the pain.

Pixie was in a frenzy of excitement as she licked at my fingers, my hand, and even my battered face.

Aunt Lou was there then. "How did that dog—?" she started to ask, but Grandpa broke in to explain.

"Forgot to close the door, and she dashed in and was on the bed quick as a wink."

I figured keeping Pixie out of my room must have been quite a chore.

"How are you, Josh?" Uncle Nat was asking.

"Okay," I said again, trying to calm Pixie down by gently stroking her so they wouldn't take her away.

"Good," said Uncle Nat. "You had us worried some. You've near slept the day away."

"You should have another pill now, Joshua," said Aunt Lou and lifted my head so I could swallow the tablet and the drink of water.

Uncle Charlie poked his head in the door. His eyes held his questions but he did not voice them. "Don't tire 'im," was all he said.

They left me then to rest and went back to the kitchen table. I could tell where they were and what they all were doing simply from the sounds in the house.

I lay quietly and let my hand rest on Pixie's head. She slept beside me, occasionally lifting her head and licking my fingers with her warm little tongue.

Soon the medicine began to take effect, but instead of sleeping deeply as I had done before, I began to do some thinking, now that the pain was dulled.

What happened anyway? Why am I here in bed? I mulled over in my mind.

Jack Berry—Jack Berry kept flashing through my thoughts but I had no idea why. What did my being in bed have to do with Jack Berry? I couldn't work my way through the fog to come up with the answer.

I lifted a hand to my face and felt the bandage on the cut over my eye. I felt my swollen nose and touched my bruised lips with my tongue.

Jack Berry, Jack Berry pounded through my brain.

Jack had been pretty nasty lately. Mad because Camellia had invited me instead of him to her house. But no girl in her right mind would invite Jack Berry to tutor her in geometry—or anything else for that matter. Jack was barely making it through his studies himself.

I tried to settle myself and piece together the events of yesterday.

I had gone to school—been teased as usual because the fellas all knew that it was the day I would again go to Camellia's house. Had I gone? I couldn't remember.

Slowly, oh, so slowly, I began to relive the day. Class by class I went over each part of it. I remembered reading—we were working on Dickens' *Christmas Carol*, it being near Christmas and all. I remembered spelling, and nearly missing the silent "e" in "maneuver." I remembered the recess break. We had wanted to play Fox and Goose but there was no clean snow to make a ring. Our whole schoolyard was a mess of trampled snow—we needed a fresh fall to make trails for the game.

I could remember the rest of my classes, right up to dismissal. I even recalled the chat with Mr. Foggelson. He said I could read the books in his library.

Did I go to Camellia's? Yes—it was beginning to take shape for me. We had tea again, as well as funny little pastries with a filling in the middle. I had nearly dropped mine in my lap. Then we studied—but mostly talked. And then I left for home—in a hurry because I was late.

Was it snowing when I left Camellia's? I couldn't remember. I left alone—to run on home—and here I was in bed with the worst headache of my life and a cut, battered face to go with it.

Jack Berry. Jack Berry.

I pushed it away. Sure, I was upset with the guy. He had been acting like a jerk lately. But it sure wasn't worth troubling myself over. I turned my eyes back to the snow and watched it fall like feathery petals. *This is great to have the freshness and cleanness for Christmas*, I thought sleepily.

"Are you feeling any better?" came a soft voice and Aunt Lou was back in my room.

I even turned my head slightly on my pillow and the pain did not sweep through me with the same intensity.

"Yeah," I answered. "Lot's better."

"Good! Are you up to visitors?"

"Sure."

Mr. Foggelson and Camellia entered my room. She looked at me and her face went white, but she came right over to my bed.

"What happened, Joshua?" she asked me, her eyes wide with the terror of it.

"I don't remember," I said honestly.

"Nothing?" asked Mr. Foggelson, as though he found that hard to believe.

"Doc said he hit his head on a rock when he fell," said Aunt Lou. "Sam took Doc back to the spot where he found Josh. The snow had covered the ground so Doc couldn't learn much, but he said there was a large rock on the ground beneath the maple tree."

Sam? Old Sam? It must be. Vaguely I remembered Sam helping me home, but nothing further would come clear to me.

"But your face—?" quizzed Mr. Foggelson. "Surely your face wasn't hurt like this in the fall."

"I don't remember," I said again, a bit stubbornly.

Camellia reached out a soft hand and gently touched the bandage over my eye.

"Does it hurt terribly, Joshua?" she asked me, wincing with the words.

"Naw," I said bravely. "I hardly feel it."

And it was true. My head had been hurting so fiercely that I hadn't really felt the cut above my eye.

"Good," she said and smiled. For a moment I didn't feel any pain at all.

"Oh!" Camellia squealed, reaching over me to gently stroke Pixie. "Your little dog. She's a darling."

Pixie responded by sending out greetings with her little pink tongue.

Camellia squealed again.

"May I hold her?" she pleaded. No wonder she got whatever she wanted from her pa.

"Sure," I said. I watched proudly as she scooped up my little dog and held her close against her cheek for a moment. Then she sat on a nearby chair with Pixie on her lap, patting the soft head and stroking the silky fur.

It was quite a sight the two of them made there together.

Mr. Foggelson broke the spell.

"We mustn't tire, Joshua, Camellia."

I noticed again the way he pronounced each syllable, and the teasing of the fellas came back to my mind. With it came the haunting rhythm of *Jack Berry, Jack Berry.* I pushed it away again and tried to thank my visitors for coming.

"Can I come again tomorrow?" Camellia begged.

"Now, Camellia," her pa objected. "You know the doctor has said that Joshua must have his rest. We do want him back in school soon."

"But, Papa—" she cajoled him, "I won't stay long. Promise."

"I'm fine," I joined in. "Likely be out of this bed by tomorrow."

"Oh, no you won't." Aunt Lou's voice came from the door. "Doc says we are to keep you here at least until Sunday afternoon."

Then she turned to Camellia and gave her a bright smile. "But I'm sure Josh would be glad for your company for twenty minutes or so—if it's okay with your folks."

Camellia rewarded her with a dazzling smile. She didn't even turn to her pa, assuming that the issue was settled.

"I'll bring a book and read to you," she promised as she put Pixie gently back on the bed beside me and the Foggelsons left my room.

One by one the family members came to see me. I guess they felt that all of them at one time would be too much for my poor head. They visited for a few minutes each, always the same questions in their eyes if not voiced. What had happened? How had I been hurt on my way home from Camellia's house? Why had Old Sam found me lying on the ground?

I still had no clear picture of the evening, only bits and pieces that made no sense. I knew that I felt anger flood through me when I thought of the night before. But I had no idea why. *Jack Berry, Jack Berry* played over and over in my head, and I couldn't imagine why that should be.

Eventually Grandpa, Uncle Charlie and Gramps went on home. I envied them their trip through the new snow, but I knew better than to coax to go with them.

Doc stopped in again before nightfall. He seemed pleased with my progress and told Aunt Lou that I could have a few more of the pills if the pain was too bad.

Uncle Nat came to chat after he had done up my evening chores. I told him I was sorry about his needing to take over for me, but he brushed it all aside, saying that the exercise was good for him.

That night we had our devotional time in my bedroom so I could share in it. In Uncle Nat's prayer he gave special thanks to God that I had been found and helped home the night before. When Aunt Lou prayed, thanking the Lord I was safe and home, I realized how worried she had been. Uncle Nat had been away at the Browns'. One of their daughters was planning a New Year's wedding, and he was counseling her and her beau. So Aunt Lou had been alone with her concern. I could imagine her going often to the front room to check the street for my return. Pixie would have been whimpering about her ankles.

I smiled as cheerfully as I could at her when she gave me a pill, tucked the blankets around me and kissed me good night. The pain in my head was much subdued. I slept.

Chapter 16

Christmas

Christmas was one of my favorite times of the year. We always went out to the farm. I don't know what part of it I liked best. I loved the smell of the spices while Aunt Lou baked savory cookies and pies. I loved the tangy odor of pine as the tree from our pasture woods was set up in a corner of the big farm kitchen, decorated with paper chains and popcorn strings. I loved the mystery of hidden gifts that a person could accidentally stumble across if he happened to be looking for something in out-of-the-way places.

I even loved the Christmas program at the church, though it took a lot of time and patience from those like Aunt Lou who worked to get it to finally come together for the night of presentation. It took a lot of hounding by the mothers—in my case, my aunt Lou—to get us to memorize the parts.

But in the end, it always came off quite well and folks enjoyed it and praised our efforts until our heads puffed up with thinking about how good we were. When it was all successfully behind us, Aunt Lou heaved a sigh of relief and put her program ideas away for another year. But she still had her books out for this year 'cause the program was yet to come.

Like I've explained, I loved the snow of Christmas. It made the world look fit to welcome the King of Kings—even if He did come as a tiny baby and likely didn't even notice if there was snow or not. But I couldn't imagine Christmas without snow. Once when a visiting speaker at our church said that there most likely was no snow in Bethlehem on the night Jesus was born, I wanted to argue back that the fellow must be wrong. To think of Christmas with no snow—a dirty, bare, sordid world to welcome the Christ-Child—just didn't seem right.

Yes, I waited every year for a Christmas snowfall. It was like a hallowed sacrament to me—the covering of the drab, ugly world with clean freshness right from the hand of God himself. The unclothed trees, the dirty rutted yard, the bare, empty fields—all were suddenly transformed into silvery, soft images, always making me think that something truly miraculous was happening before my very eyes.

I had been allowed to return to school the Tuesday after my accident—or whatever it was. My face was still a bit swollen and my eye discolored, but other than that, I felt quite good. The doc insisted that I not be active in any of the boys' games, so I stayed in at recess time. I felt like a jerk—like some kind of sissy. But it did prove to be an opportunity to spend some time with one of Mr. Foggelson's books. He brought it for me and kept it locked in a corner cupboard. He brought it out only after the rest of the students had left the room, and returned it to the cupboard again before he rang the bell.

My head gradually stopped aching and I seemed to be back to normal. I felt awful about Uncle Nat doing my chores, but the doc insisted that for at least two weeks I was to do nothing strenuous. Two weeks would take us past Christmas.

I still had this troubled feeling about Jack Berry. He wasn't at school either, and word had it that he was down sick with the flu. That would keep him out of my hair for a while. By the time he was back, my eye and bruised nose and lips would be back to normal again and he would not have further occasion to goad me.

Camellia kept fussing over me. She said she felt to blame, seeing that I was on my way home from her house—but that was ridiculous. The attention was embarrassing, but sort of special, too.

As I watched this Christmas quickly approaching, I was filled with all kinds of mixed emotions.

I had been storing away every nickel and dime I could get my hands on for shopping for my Christmas gifts. It would have worked out just fine, too, if Camellia hadn't entered my life when she did.

Most every day I went back to my dresser drawer and counted those coins. They sure didn't multiply any. I still had the same four dollars and fifteen cents. I'd figured on paper just what I would get for each family member and had it all worked out just fine until I decided that the only right thing to do was to get Camellia a gift as well. I mean, she had been so nice to me and all.

I reworked my list a dozen times but I couldn't get it to work out.

If I'd been healthy, I mean, if Doc hadn't made his silly pronouncement that I wasn't to "exert" myself, I could've been hustling around town looking for odd jobs. But with things as they were, there wasn't a hope in the world that I could get ahold of any more money before Christmas. So I wanted Christmas to come, but I didn't know what to do about gifts.

I window-shopped one more time and came up with decisions about family gifts that would leave me with fifty-five cents! With excitement coursing through my veins and joy in my heart, I went looking for a gift for Camellia.

The joy didn't last long. There was nothing that would do for a girl like Camellia that could be purchased for a mere fifty-five cents. Nothing.

I went home with a heavy heart, my feet dragging across the snow-covered ground.

Pixie met me at the door. I pulled her into my arms and held her close while she licked my face. *Pixie!* I could give my dog to Camellia! There was likely nothing on earth I could give her that she would like more. I remembered the time when she had come to read to me when I was in bed.

She had loved my little dog and never tired of holding her or of watching her playful antics or her puppy tricks.

But how can I give Pixie away? I moaned. Never was a fella so torn. I loved Pixie more than I had ever loved anything—except for family, that is. As a matter-of-fact, it was awfully easy to think of Pixie as family. I held her so close just thinking about it that she started to whine.

But Camellia? She was pretty special too, and if you really cared about someone, weren't you supposed to put that person's wants and needs before your own?

I was still battling it through in my mind, this way and that, when it dawned on me that Camellia said she couldn't have a dog because of her ma's allergies. I hugged Pixie even tighter and breathed a prayer of thanks.

Boy, was I glad for that allergy. I sure wouldn't have been able to decide that tough one on my own.

Without even knowing, Uncle Nat solved my problem about a gift—though he did sort of leave it until the last minute.

I knew he had been secretly working on a cedar chest for Aunt Lou for her Christmas present. He kept it hidden at the farm, and he slipped out and spent time on it for an hour or so when he'd finished his pastoral visits and duties.

The first weekend I was allowed to go home to the farm—the only weekend before the Christmas break—Uncle Nat came out on Saturday morning, determined to get the chest finished.

It was a beautiful piece of work. Uncle Nat didn't have many fancy tools, but he had a lot of love for Aunt Lou. He did want the chest to be just right, so he toiled over it, careful to make every board fit perfectly.

It smelled good, too. I loved the smell of the cedar.

I guess I said some nice things about the chest and about the smell of the wood, for Uncle Nat, without even looking up from his work, said, "There's a bit of lumber left over, Josh, some board scraps and things. You're welcome to them if you'd like them for anything."

"Thanks," I said without too much enthusiasm, "but I

wouldn't know what to do with 'em."

"You could always make a little jewelry box or a treasure box."

I was about to ask him who that would be for, knowing that Aunt Lou already had a jewelry box, when I thought of Camellia.

"Could you help me?" I asked instead, unable to hide the eagerness in my voice.

"I guess I could—I don't think it'd take too much time."

I couldn't believe my good luck. I went right to work on it. With Uncle Nat's guidance in measuring and sawing, and help from Uncle Charlie in the sanding and Gramps in the varnishing, I got the small box finished in time for Christmas. It looked just fine. I could hardly wait for Camellia to see it.

That Sunday, December twenty-second, we had our Christmas program in the evening. I had hoped Camellia would attend. I mean, she knew I had an important part in it and had been studying on it for weeks. But she wasn't there.

I tried to put her from my mind and think about other things—like how my lines went—but I have to admit that I was deeply disappointed.

The program went all right. I can't say it was perfect. But it was close enough for folks to overlook the little things and compliment us all on our efforts after it was over.

Aunt Lou went home tired that evening and placed her hat on the hall closet shelf.

"I'm glad that's over," she said with a sigh as she always did, and Uncle Nat gave her an impromptu hug.

"You did a great job," he assured her.

The next morning Aunt Lou was back in true form again, scurrying around doing the work of three people. Christmas was just two days off.

The next morning I took my four dollars and fifteen cents and went to the store to purchase the family presents I had planned to buy in the first place since I didn't need the fifty-five cents for Camellia. Then borrowing some bits of paper from Aunt Lou, I got them all wrapped up.

I had to ask help from Aunt Lou in wrapping Camellia's present. I wanted Camellia's gift to look especially nice.

I took the gift over to Camellia's house when I knew she would be off to Miss Thompson's house for her weekly piano lesson. I gave the package to Mrs. Foggelson and asked her to place it under their tree on Christmas Eve, and she promised to do that for me.

I felt real good about it all. When I got back home I gave Pixie a big hug, feeling that I hadn't compromised a bit.

On the twenty-fourth we were up early and packed into the cutter with boxes and bags stacked in all around us. We were off to the farm for our annual Christmas festivities. I had never called them "festivities" before, but that was what Camellia's ma called them.

"Where will you celebrate your Christmas 'festivities'?" she had asked me.

At first I didn't know what she meant.

"Don't you celebrate Christmas?" she asked, looking puzzled.

"Oh, sure," I said, the light beginning to dawn. "We always go to the farm and have it all together."

"The farm?"

"My grandpa's. Him and Uncle Charlie and Gramps live there. Uncle Nat and Aunt Lou and me—and I—go on out there and join 'em."

"That's nice," she said, "—a real old-fashioned Christmas."

"Yeah," I answered, "yeah, a real old-fashioned Christmas."

So now we were on our way to our "festivities" and I was all excited inside, just like I was every year.

It was a good Christmas, too. We had the best-tasting turkey I can ever remember, and I got the nicest presents, too. There was a new store-bought sweater from Grandpa, a real fishing rod from Gramps, a shirt from Uncle Nat and Aunt Lou that she had made, and a brand-new five-blade knife from Uncle Charlie. There was even a surprise gift. A large, colorfully illustrated book from Camellia titled *How the World Began* was full of the strangest pictures and diagrams. I could hardly wait to read it and find out what it was all about.

I wondered what she had thought of the "treasure box" from me. I sure hoped she liked it.

After the paper had been pulled from all of the presents and each one had told the others how much we liked their gifts, Uncle Nat went out and brought in the chest for Aunt Lou. It was about all that one man could carry, and when she heard the thumping behind her and wheeled to see what was going on, her breath caught in a little gasp and tears filled her eyes.

She nearly bowled Uncle Nat over when she threw herself into his arms and wept against his shoulder. I kept checking her face to be sure, but the tears were for joy, not sadness. I had never seen a woman quite so "joyous" before.

"It's lovely! It's perfect!" she kept saying over and over, and Uncle Nat just held her close and patted her shoulder.

Then Aunt Lou turned to all of us. The tears were still sliding down her cheeks, but she had the brightest smile that I have ever seen her wear.

"I already have plans for its use," she said, "and I can hardly wait to fill it. The chest is going to be for our baby's things."

A real commotion took place then. Everyone seemed to be hugging everyone else, and more than just Aunt Lou were shedding tears. I couldn't make much sense out of any of it until I heard Grandpa asking, "When? When?"

"In July," said Aunt Lou. "Oh, Pa, I'm so happy I could just burst!"

I understood it then. My aunt Lou was having a baby! I was getting a new cousin. Imagine that! Me, a cousin! I'd be able to help take care of it and everything.

With a whoop I was across the room and hugging Aunt Lou as tightly as I dared. I wasn't sure, but I thought there might be some tears on my cheeks, too.

Chapter 17

Back to School

I was anxious to get back to school again after our Christmas break, and not just to find out what Camellia had thought of my Christmas gift. I also wanted to tell the fellas about the nice gifts I had gotten and how much stuffed turkey and apple pie I had eaten and all. It was the same every year.

I guess they were just as eager to share their Christmas news—they were all there waiting at the corner of the schoolyard when I arrived.

We all talked at once and no one really listened much, but I did get the feeling that they all were pretty happy with the Christmas they had just shared with their family.

Willie had some other news too. Jack Berry had dropped out of school. It shouldn't have surprised us any, and I guess that it didn't much. I mean, Jack Berry had never been fond of school. It was his pa's idea that he keep on going. Well, with him missing so many days before Christmas with the flu and all, I guess Jack decided he didn't want to work so hard to catch up to the class, so he finally talked his pa into letting him quit.

I wouldn't have said so to the fellas, but I wasn't going to do much crying over Jack being gone. He had been acting so nasty of late that I figured school, at least for me, would be a better place without him. No, I wasn't prepared to be missing Jack Berry much at all. I was content to let the matter drop.

I felt pretty good about life when Camellia told me she really liked my Christmas gift. She said she was going to keep her hankies in it and, not wanting to argue none with her, I didn't tell her I thought hankies to be rather strange "treasures." They sure weren't treasures in my book.

I knew Aunt Lou wouldn't be too happy with me spreading the news of the coming baby among all of my school chums yet, so I held my tongue; but it was awfully hard to keep the excitement to myself. We had never welcomed a little one into our family since I had arrived, and of course I didn't remember anything about what happened at my own coming.

There were some days when Aunt Lou didn't feel too well. I could tell it by looking at her, but she never made any mention of the fact. I guess Uncle Nat and I were both watching for signs. I tried to keep the woodbox a little fuller and made sure there was plenty of water on hand from our yard pump. Uncle Nat was watching for ways he could ease her load as well, but she usually laughed at our anxieties and assured us that she was just fine. She did look a little tired at times, though, and I knew she skipped breakfast some mornings.

Still, things seemed to settle down and the household pretty much ran as it had before, except for the underlying current of anticipation that we all felt.

I started "tutoring" Camellia again. We spent most of the time poring over her pa's books, discussing interesting things that we found.

I had read the book that Camellia gave me for Christmas. It was rather a strange one. Parts of it I couldn't make much sense of. I mean, it said, bold as brass, that man sort of oozed into being, coming up out of the muck and mire and then went from a primitive stage to a more progressive stage of development. As I say, it puzzled me at first because I knew how man really had come into being, and I scratched my head a bit until I realized that the book must be some new sort of book of fancy. Then I settled back and tried to let the imaginings of this writer interest me.

It was quite a tale. All about how this new man creature "evolved" until finally he discovered how to walk up on his two hind feet and use his forefeet to grip things. He did this so much that finally his forefeet turned into fingers for gripping, and then he learned new skills and lost his shaggy fur so he had to make clothes to protect himself and build homes to live in and plant crops for food that he learned to store and preserve.

Even though the whole book was a fairy tale sort of thing, I couldn't make out the reasoning behind it. What I mean is, each stage that this man "advanced" seemed to bring him a lot more troubles and complications instead of simplifying things for him. So why did the teller-of-the-tale bother with the advancing?

It must have been that some folks thought it made interesting "supposing," but I preferred fanciful stories to make a bit of sense. Anyway, I guessed that the Foggelsons liked this kind of fairy tale and wanted me to become acquainted with it, too. I certainly didn't plan to tell Camellia what I thought of her book.

Then one day when we were reading some of Mr. Foggelson's other books, we came on the same kind of tale again.

"Here's another one," I mumbled more to myself than to Camellia.

"Another what?" she asked.

"Another fairy tale about man creepin' up outta particles of something or other and startin' to live on his own."

"Joshua," said Camellia, surprise in her voice, "that's not a fairy tale."

I just looked at her. I didn't know what to say.

"What do *you* call it?" I finally asked, thinking that Camellia must know a new word for a fanciful tale that I didn't know.

"Evolution," she answered, as though surprised I didn't know the word already.

"Evolution. Oh!"

I let the matter drop, but I repeated the word several times to myself so I wouldn't forget it. I intended to look it up when I got home so that next time I could impress the Foggelsons by naming the tale by its proper name.

Even before I sat down with my cookies and milk when I got home, I looked up the word. Old Webster was a good friend of mine, and I guess I depended on him to know the meaning of most every word there was. I found "evolution" and his meaning for it. Webster said a number of things about evolution that didn't seem to fit. He talked about development and growth, about movement of troops in marching or on the battlefield, and about arithmetic and algebra. None of those meanings made sense when I connected them with the Foggelson books. Then he said, "The gradual development or descent of forms of life from simple or low organized types consisting of a single cell."

I still couldn't understand it. I tossed the words around in my mind all the time that I was choring, but I never did get them sorted out.

After supper was over and we'd had our Bible reading together, I again pulled out Webster's Dictionary. I read it over again, but I still couldn't get the meaning, so I let my eyes travel down the page a bit and checked some other words, hoping that that would help. "Evolutional" was pertaining to evolution. That sure didn't help me any, and then I read through the lengthy explanation of "evolutionist" until I came to the part that said, "The theory that man is a development from a lower order of creation; a teacher or advocate of Darwinism."

I read it again. Surely no one really believed that man "developed" that way. Why, that wasn't anywhere near what the Bible said. I may not have listened to preachers as much as I should have, but I had listened enough to know how man came into being, and how they had gotten to their sorry state of sinfulness, too.

Before closing Webster up again, I got a stub of a pencil and a piece of paper and wrote down the words from the printed page. I needed to do some thinking about this and talk to Mr. Foggelson and Camellia. Did the fact that they weren't churchgoers mean that they had never heard how things *really* happened? I couldn't believe that someone could have missed out so completely on the facts.

I wasn't sure whether I should make use of Uncle Nat's help on this or not, but I hated to bother him with my problem. I knew he had plenty of his own—and other peoples'.

Gramps and I had a chance for some checker games that weekend. The weather was stormy and cold, and it didn't make much sense to go out in it unless one had a good reason for going. So Uncle Charlie and Grandpa spent some time working on harness mending and drinking coffee, and Gramps and I read and played checkers.

Gramps beat me, which wasn't unusual. He had won three games before I pushed the board back a bit and stood to stretch.

"Mind not on the game, Joshua?" he quizzed me.

I grinned. "You 'most always beat me," I answered good-naturedly. "Can't always blame it on my mind bein' else-where."

"No not always—but this time I think we can."

I stopped my grinning. "Maybe so," I admitted, and sat back down again.

"Just thinkin' on some of my studies. Been reading some real interestin' books. Lots of new things to learn—new ideas. Some of them I understand, some I don't."

"Like?" said Gramps.

"Well, like—like—well, evolution."

I expected I would have to stop and explain the word to Gramps, and my hand started into my pocket to pull out the paper I had written Webster's words on, but Gramps surprised me.

"Hogwash!" he said with sort of a snort.

My eyes popped wide open.

"Pure hogwash," Gramps said again, and I knew he felt pretty sure of himself.

"What's it all about anyway?" I asked him.

Gramps didn't even hesitate.

"This man, Darwin, got these funny ideas of where man came from—where everything came from," he said. "He saw the similarity in the animals and birds and fish, and decided that they had a common source."

I nodded.

"Well, he was right," went on Gramps to my surprise; "they do have a common source. A common Creator. Only thing is Darwin got mixed up about the beginnings. He thought that because this 'common' bond, this thread, ran through all creatures, the one came from the other. He decided that he knew more about things than anyone else who ever lived and threw out what the Good Book said about God creating all things in the beginning. Got himself in a heap of trouble, because try as he did to make all the pieces fit, he never did get them untangled.

"But others jumped on that theory and they too kept trying to come up with 'proofs' for what they thought they found. They haven't let it die yet. Been lots of books written on it and some places now teach Darwin's theory as if it were fact. Don't let it throw you, Joshua. It still is theory. No facts have proved it yet—and they never will. What God has said still stands. Remember that. God was the only one around at the time, so I'm willing to take His word on just how it all happened."

I guess I took a deep breath. Gramps stopped his talking and his eyes pinned me down.

"That new teacher been trying to teach you evolution?"

"Not in school, no," I said quickly.

"Then where'd you get this stuff?"

"Camellia gave me a book for Christmas an'—" I hated to lay the blame on Camellia.

Gramps just nodded.

"Her pa is letting me read his library books. I found the same thing in them, and Camellia says that—"

"Don't you believe it," Gramps cut in. "Not one word of it."

I nodded and swallowed hard. It was a relief to me to have some solid ground under my feet again.

With my beliefs about creation and the Creator securely intact again, I felt an obligation to pass on my knowledge to Camellia.

The next Thursday when we settled ourselves to study after having our tea and those messy little pastries, I brought up the subject.

"You know those books," I began, trying to choose my words carefully, "well, they are a bit mixed up on things."

"What books?" she asked me.

I didn't want to come across as a know-it-all, but I did feel that Camellia should know the truth.

"The ones on evolution," I said hesitantly.

"Mixed up? How?" she asked.

"That's not the way things really happened," I stated firmly. "The Bible has it all in here," and I pulled my Bible out from under my sweater and proceeded to open it to Genesis, chapter one.

"Oh, Josh," Camellia said, playfully pushing at my hand that held the Book. "Don't tease."

I blinked.

Camellia was entertaining herself in silvery gales of laughter.

"I'm not teasin'," I finally said, my voice low and serious.

Camellia's laughter died then and she looked at me, her face wearing a look of total disbelief.

"You're not?"

"No, I'm not. See? It's all right here. Nothing evolved. God created everything."

"You don't really believe that?"

"I do—I most certainly do. And you would, too, if you'd just read what it says. See—"

"But it doesn't make sense. I mean—"

"*Evolution* doesn't make sense," I countered rather hotly. "Why would things 'evolve' when their present state was not nearly as demanding? Why—"

"Oh, Joshua—think! Don't just fall dumbly for those old superstitions that have been passed down from generation to generation. We are enlightened now! No one who is a scholar believes that Bible gibberish."

I looked at her in silence, my thumb still held in the page I had wanted to show her.

"You know what it says?" I finally asked.

"Of course I know what it says. Papa taught me all about the false statements that are in there so I might know how to refute them."

"You don't believe the Bible?" I asked in amazement. I could not understand how anyone could possibly know what was written in its pages and still not believe what it said.

Camellia stood up and came slowly to me. She was no longer smiling, but she had a soft, pleading look about her now, like a woman placating a spoiled or sensitive child.

"Look, Joshua," she said, "we understand that this is hard for you, being raised in the church and—and—well, we are willing to take it slowly—to help you to understand. That's why Papa has given you the use of his library. With scientific data at your disposal, you will discover the truth for yourself. You have a good mind, Joshua. Papa is most pleased with it. I am proud of you. You can be anything you want to be. There is no limit, Joshua."

"I'm gonna be a preacher," I said quietly.

"But *anybody* can be a preacher," Camellia moaned. "Can't you see?"

I shut my Bible with a slam I had never used on it before and immediately felt ashamed of myself. Unconsciously I reopened it and closed it tenderly.

"I'm afraid I don't see," I said to Camellia.

"Well, Papa said that you have potential. More potential than any student he has ever had. He will help you make something worthwhile of yourself if only—"

"An' you were helping him?" I asked coldly.

"Of course." The words were out before Camellia realized what she'd said. She caught herself and flushed. "Well, not the way you mean. I like you, Joshua, I do—"

"I think I'd better go," I said, feeling all mixed up inside. I couldn't understand all of this, but I didn't like it. Not one bit. I moved to the door, but Camellia was there before me.

She faced me, with cheeks flushed and her eyes sparking angrily. Even then I was aware of how pretty she was.

"Joshua," she said, "if you go like this—just up and walk out in a rage—can't you see what it will do to my father? Hasn't he suffered enough already? He lost his position in his last school—a good position—just because he tried to help some capable students understand science, true science. And now you are going to—to spurn his help and—"

I had stopped. I couldn't very well push her aside and force my way out of her home.

"Don't you see," she went on. "He just wants to help you."

"By takin' away the truth—and makin' me believe a lie?"

"I can't believe this, Joshua," she said hotly. "You have a good mind. How can you just accept everything that they tell you—without thinking it through or anything."

"But don't you see," I replied, "that is what you've done. I mean, just because you love your pa, you believe whatever he tells you without even having proof. The Bible has been proved over and over, and it never comes up short with pieces all missin' and—"

Camellia moved away from the door. Her eyes were dark with rage.

"If you go now," she said through tight lips, "don't ever come back."

I nodded my head, my throat workin' hard on a swallow. I wanted to invite her to church. I wanted to say that I'd pray that she might learn the truth. I wanted to say that I was sorry—for—for how everything had turned out, but I couldn't find my voice to say anything, so I just nodded and left.

That heavy lump in my chest stayed with me as I made my way home. My feet dragged, and the short distance had never seemed so long before.

Chapter 18

Hard Days

The next morning, after a restless night, I wished with all of my heart that I could just stay in bed and not ever go to school again. I knew Aunt Lou would soon be in my room fussing over me if I was even late getting up, so I reluctantly crawled out and made my usual preparations. I sure didn't want Aunt Lou fretting about me for fear it might cause some kind of harm to the coming baby.

I dressed and washed at the kitchen basin and slicked down my hair good enough to do. We had our breakfast together, Uncle Nat telling Aunt Lou his plans for the day. I was glad I didn't need to enter the conversation much.

In no hurry at all to get to school, I sort of dawdled along until I heard the bell ring. I had never been late for school before and I found myself running now. I didn't want a "tardy" mark on my report card.

Most of the kids had already hung up their coats and shoved and pushed their way into the classroom by the time I arrived, puffing from my run. I hurriedly threw my jacket at my hanger and, fortunately, it stuck. I picked up my books and my lunch bucket and hurried to my place. I almost ran smack into Camellia in the hall. I guess we both got red. Me, from embarrassment. From the way she sniffed and flung back her long, silken hair, I guessed her redness was from anger.

I stumbled my way to my desk and got out my Dickens like I was supposed to do.

There were no flashing smiles across the room, no waiting at the door just to walk out into the schoolyard with me. I tried not to even look her way, and I suppose she tried not to look mine.

Mr. Foggelson did not call on me to recite or give an answer all day long. In fact, I might as well not have been there for all I was noticed.

The fellas must have realized something was up. At recess time their teasing took a new tack. I tried to ignore them, "What happened, Josh—drop all her books in the snow?" and so on. I tried to ignore them, but it was pretty hard to hide the fact that things were different now.

When school was over for the day, I breathed a sigh of relief, ready to hurriedly slip from the school building and run for home. But Mr. Foggelson's voice stopped me. He hadn't used the raised eyebrow trick, and I had been sure I was going to be able to slip off without a confrontation. Now his soft-spoken call of my name stopped me mid-stride.

I turned slowly, half hoping I was only hearing things. I wasn't. There stood my teacher beside my desk, the chalk brush in his hand and his eyes on me.

I retraced my steps slowly.

"You—you wished to see me, sir?" I said after swallowing two or three times.

"Yes, Joshua." He pointed to my seat.

I sat down, somewhat glad that I didn't need to stand. On the other hand, I knew I wouldn't be able to bolt for the door from a sitting position, and I sure did wish I could bolt.

Mr. Foggelson laid aside the brush and pulled out a handkerchief to wipe his hands. The actions were slow and deliberate and I waited, wishing to get this over.

"Camellia tells me that you and she had an unfortunate little misunderstanding last evening," he said slowly. He waited for me to acknowledge his words and I finally found my voice.

"I don't think so, sir," I said respectfully.

His eyebrows shot up.

"You didn't have a misunderstanding?"

"No, sir. I think we understood one another very well."

He paused and stared at me. I tried not to let my eyes waver.

"You'll have to explain that, Joshua," he said then. "I don't believe I follow you."

"Well," I said, shuffling my feet under my desk and dropping my gaze, "Camellia believes that stuff about evolution, and I believe what the Bible says."

"Have you studied evolution, Joshua?" he asked me, knowing that I would have to say no.

"No, sir. Not really. But I've read enough—"

"Perhaps you are making your judgment too hastily," went on Mr. Foggelson reasonably. "Don't you feel that you should acquaint yourself with all of the facts before making your decision?"

I had dropped my gaze but I raised my eyes again so I could look squarely at him. I tried not to flinch.

"No, sir," I said, rather quietly.

"And why not?" he quizzed me. "Are you afraid of the truth?"

I answered that one quickly.

"No, sir."

"Then why did you refuse to look at what other learned scholars have arrived at after years and years of scientific study deductions?"

"Because—" I swallowed again, "because, sir, it disagrees with the Holy Scriptures."

"Have you ever considered that the 'Holy Scriptures,' as you call it, could be wrong? That it could be a mere invention of man to satisfy his superstitious need for a god to cling to?"

"No, sir."

"Then perhaps, Joshua, it would do you well to carefully

consider the possibility. How do you know that your 'Bible' is as accurate as you have been made to believe? How do you know that it isn't a book of fairy tales? Do you have proof, beyond all doubt?"

I didn't answer. I just sat there and shuffled my feet and swallowed and awkwardly thumbed the pages of my geography book.

"I want you to think about it, Joshua. A good mind is not to be wasted. I would feel a failure if you, my best student, closed the covers of scientific books because you dared not challenge the teachings that you have had thrust upon you since babyhood. If the Bible is really true, then it should bear the scrutiny, right?"

That sounded reasonable. I nodded dumbly.

"Well, then," said Mr. Foggelson, giving me the token of a smile, "I am glad we have had this talk. My library is still at your disposal. I hope you will use it, and open your mind up to all truth."

He nodded and I understood that meant I was dismissed. I gathered up my books and stood to my feet.

"Good night, sir," I had the presence of mind to mumble and left the room, gathering momentum with each step.

A lot of troubled thoughts were tumbling around in my head, but of one thing I was sure. I would not be going back to the Foggelsons' to use the books in the library. There was too much in them that I wasn't ready for yet. Someday— maybe someday I would need to grapple with the theories they presented as fact, but not now. I wasn't ready to face them head-on, and I had the sense to know it.

And I wouldn't be going back to "tutor" Camellia either. The tutoring was just a ruse. I had liked her. Had enjoyed hearing her laugh, her chatter, had liked to watch her toss her mane of shiny hair, had found her exciting and interesting, but I wouldn't be going back. She left me with such confusing thoughts when she challenged my belief in the Bible, my desire to be a minister. No, I would not spend time with Camellia again.

And the tea and pastries I could sure do without. Aunt Lou's milk and cookies were far more filling.

No! I was most definite in my decision. I would not be going back to the Foggelson house.

Chapter 19

Spring

I was glad to put the difficult months of January and February behind me. By March I was feeling more comfortable at school. Mr. Foggelson had obviously given up on me, for he never asked me to come over to the house or stay and chat after class. I felt sorry about it in a way, but I was relieved, too.

He hadn't given up on some of his theories though, about "religion" being an escape for shallow minds or evolution being the "true" science. Often he inserted sarcastic little comments into his class lectures. At first I could often feel Camellia's eyes on me at such times, but then she too seemed to put me out of her mind entirely.

Word began to circulate through town that Jack Berry was doing a lot of visiting at Camellia's house. I don't know why that bothered me, but the haunting old chant of *Jack Berry, Jack Berry* was hammering away in my brain again. I tried hard to shove it aside but it kept hanging in there. I didn't understand it. Why was it haunting me again?

By the time March arrived, things had pretty well returned to normal—that is for Willie, Avery and me. We tried a bit of kite flying on the windy days—and there were lots of them. Not all of the snow had left us yet, but that didn't slow us down none. We were used to trying to fly kites with snow still on the ground. Truth was, I guess we just couldn't wait for real spring to come.

It was obvious now to the entire congregation that Aunt Lou was expecting her first baby. When news started to circulate about the coming big event, young women exclaimed with red-flushed cheeks, girls tittered and got all excited and matronly ladies had lots and lots of advice to give to the mother-to-be. Aunt Lou took it all good-naturedly. I think she loved the attention. I do know for sure she was plumb excited about that baby. Already she was busy filling the cedar chest with all sorts of special little tiny garments. Made me think about my ma—had it been that way with her when she knew I was on the way?

All the menfolk at the farm were talking about that baby, too. Grandpa was busy fashioning a wooden cradle, and every weekend when I went home, he would show me how far along he was on his project. He worked on it in the near-empty parlor, and it was coming along very nicely, too.

Uncle Charlie had a project of his own. He was making a woven hamper for Aunt Lou to keep all of the baby's soiled laundry until washday. He couldn't do too much with wood, he said, but that laundry hamper sure did look nice.

Even Gramps was busy. His project I found the most interesting of all. He was piecing together a quilt just big enough for the baby's bed.

"If your great-grandmother were here, she would insist on a homemade quilt for that little bed," Gramps told me. "She could do the most beautiful stitching, your great-grandmother. Well, I can't do it as fine as she could have done, but that baby is going to have a quilt anyway," and he went to town and purchased materials and started to work on that quilt. I guess he must have watched Great-grandmother do the job many times, for he seemed to know just how to get on with it.

I wanted to do something for the new baby, too, but I didn't know just what it would be. I couldn't work with tools much, and I didn't have any idea how to weave. I wasn't about to have the fellas find out I was sewing—I'd had my fill of teasing for the year—so quilting was out of the question. I finally decided to see what I could find for odd jobs so I might earn myself a bit of money to buy something for the baby.

There really wasn't that much opportunity for paying work in our small town, but I did hang around the stores all I could and let it be known that I was willing to run errands or do some sweeping up or whatever else came about.

It was while I was sweeping the sidewalk in front of the downtown hotel one sunny spring day in mid-April that Mrs. Foggelson came along. She smiled nicely at me and I doffed my cap like I had been taught and smiled back at her. After all, she had been awfully kind to me.

"Good afternoon, Joshua," she said, and then remarked about what a fine day we were having.

I agreed and moved aside so she could pass more easily. It was then that I noticed that her arms were full of packages. I was finished with my sweeping and had a few extra minutes before choring and I knew what Aunt Lou would wish me to do.

"I just need to give Mr. Powell back his broom," I said to Mrs. Foggelson, "an' I'll be glad to help you home with your packages."

"How thoughtful of you, Joshua," she said, giving me another smile.

I ran to report to Mr. Powell and was soon back out on the sidewalk again. I eased some of the packages from Mrs. Foggelson's arms and we started out together.

"I've missed you, Joshua," she said to me.

I didn't know quite how to respond so I said nothing, just sort of pretended I didn't hear her. We walked along in silence for some minutes, talking only now and then about the sunshine, the spots of new green grass and Mrs. Jones's daffodils that were nodding golden heads in the slight breeze.

We were almost home when Mrs. Foggelson spoke again.

"I know that it must have been very difficult for you, Joshua. I'm sorry about it."

I was about to assure Mrs. Foggelson that I did not blame her in any way for what had happened, but she went on in a quiet, sad voice, "When I married Mr. Foggelson I was a believer, too. I wasn't strong like you, Joshua. I didn't stand up to him. His arguments sounded so logical, so profound. How could I, a mere girl turning woman, with no education higher than the eighth grade, possibly know more than this man who had trained in one of the country's best colleges? I gave in and I shouldn't have. I lost far more than I realized at the time."

I just sort of stumbled to a stop and looked in the sad face of this distressed woman. I had no words of comfort or of counsel.

"But it's not too late," I finally stammered.

"Oh, it is, Joshua, it is," she said with a resigned sigh.

"But—" I started to protest, wishing that Uncle Nat was there and hardly able to wait to get home to talk to him about Mrs. Foggelson and her problem.

She stopped me.

"I have shared my little secret with you, Joshua, because I know what you are feeling—because I admire you for standing strong—but, please, please, keep our secret. Promise me, Joshua?"

I had to promise. Standing there facing Mrs. Foggelson with the tears just ready to slip from her eyes and course down her cheeks, I could do nothing else. But it was a hard promise for me to make. Now I would be unable to tell Uncle Nat or Aunt Lou about her, about how she needed to be helped to understand that she could still come back to the church, and to her God.

"I—I promise," I reluctantly agreed.

She lifted a gloved hand to carefully wipe away the unwanted tear and then smiled again. No one would have known that she had been so sad-looking just a moment before.

"Thank you, Joshua," she said in almost a whisper. "Thank you for sharing my load—and my groceries."

We were at her door then, and I waited while she took in the things she was carrying and returned to take the parcels from me.

She smiled at me again and said another thank you and I doffed my cap and hurried back down the walk. I didn't especially want to meet Camellia or Mr. Foggelson.

I was just leaving the yard when I unexpectedly ran into Jack Berry. And I mean just that. I wasn't paying very close attention to where I was going, I guess, and I swung around some shrubbery and smacked right into someone starting up the Foggelson walk. We both started to mumble our apologies and then Jack got a look at who he was talking to.

Before I knew what had happened he had a fist full of my shirt front and he was pulling me toward him with his face going red with anger.

"You been sneakin' around callin' on Camellia?" he hissed.

I attempted to get my shirt front back.

"I have not," I hissed back, and jerked on Jack's hand.

"Are you sure?" he shot back at me.

"I don't lie an' you know it!" I spat at him. "Let go a my shirt."

He did let go but his face was still red and angry.

"I'll ask Camellia," he assured me, "an' if you have, you're gonna be sorry. Next time you won't get off with just a bump on your poor dumb head."

I pushed past Jack and started for home, inwardly raging. My shirt wasn't damaged badly but one button hung loose. Stupid Jack Berry! *I never did care too much for the guy*, I told myself, but I quickly amended the thought. It wasn't true. There had been a time when I counted Jack Berry as one of my friends.

But that was before Camellia had come to town and he had gone off with his craziness over the girl. He acted like one who had lost his mind or something, the way he carried on. Well, he could have Camellia. I didn't care. No, that wasn't quite true, either. I still thought she was the prettiest girl I had ever seen. I still enjoyed her silvery laughter and the toss of her coppery curls. I still prayed for her every night when I said my prayers. I prayed for her pa, too, and now that I knew the situation I would pray for her ma most of all.

I continued on home, still riled by my encounter and trying to sort through the whole silly mess. Life sure could get complicated. How did one ever get it all put together anyway?

In the back of my mind the old chant started again. *Jack Berry, Jack Berry.* The whole thing just made me feel madder. And now I was a little late for choring as well. I knew Aunt Lou would understand when I told her my reason, but that wouldn't help my chores to get done any faster.

I was just passing by the schoolyard when I met Old Sam. He was stumbling along, the coat Uncle Nat had found for him open and flopping back and forth with each staggering step. It looked to me like it had all of the buttons torn from it, but Sam didn't seem to mind. He was muttering or humming to himself and clutching a nearly empty bottle close against his chest as though he was afraid someone might try to wrest it from him.

He waved his bottle in the air when he saw me. I guess he knew it was safe enough. I wouldn't be wanting it.

"Hi, Joshsh," he slurred his greeting to me and hiccupped.

"Hi, Sam," I answered without stopping.

"Now, don' ya go fall ag'in, Joshsh," he said and chuckled. Without even meaning to I looked aside and there, sure enough, was the big rock that I was said to have hit my head on.

Jack Berry, Jack Berry chanted my mind. What had Jack just said? Next time I wouldn't get off with just a bump to my dumb head. Suddenly, without warning, everything fell into place. *It was Jack's voice I heard that night!* We had fought. He had hit me and I had stumbled. That was when I must have hit my head. And good old Jack Berry had run off and left me there, knowing full well I might die of cold before I was ever found.

An anger took hold of me such as I had never felt before. It was all that I could do to keep myself from turning around and heading straight back to the Foggelsons' to confront the dirty, yellow good-for-nothing Berry right on the spot and make him pay for what he'd done.

I likely would have, too, had it not been for Aunt Lou. Somehow the fact that she needed me, needed me to haul the wood and water, and needed to not worry about where I was, kept me heading for home. There was no way I wanted to cause any anxiety for her—especially with the birth of that baby getting closer and closer.

Chapter 20

Pain

Spring slid from April through May and into June. After everything that had happened to me, the days seemed lazy and uneventful. At school, Mr. Foggelson's attitude toward me was to either ignore or avoid me, and I preferred it that way. Camellia was too busy telling secrets to the other girls to pay much attention to any of us fellas. We all knew that Jack Berry was still a frequent visitor at Camellia's house.

I no longer cared. I still burned with anger every time I thought about Jack. Since my memory had come back, I had never discussed with anyone the details of the night he had laid ambush for me. Maybe I was afraid someone would try to talk me out of my anger, I don't know. Anyway, I nursed my anger and conjured up all sorts of evil and torturous things that I hoped would one day happen to Jack Berry.

By June the sun became warm in the sky. Old Sam no longer wore his ragged, buttonless coat, not even in the cooler evenings. Uncle Nat still watched out for him, but Sam seemed to fare well enough. I had the impression that he was without any normal feelings for hot or cold, right or wrong, and I dismissed him from my mind. Uncle Nat didn't though—not for a moment. I couldn't really understand his deep concern. The old man seemed content enough in his drunken state of fantasy.

June arrived bringing yellow splashes of sunlight, young

rhubarb pushing its way up in a corner of Aunt Lou's garden, and new calves and foals frisking in the fields along the road leading to the farm. I was thinking that spring must be about the best time of the whole year—and then I thought about harvest and knew I really liked that even better. And then of course there was Christmas ... Well, anyway, I liked spring a lot.

I had some extra chores after school each day, but they didn't bother me none. It stayed light much longer now and so choring was no problem. The extras involved Aunt Lou's garden patch. The long rows of vegetables were sending up little spikes of green that gradually unfurled to be a pair of leaves, then four, then six, until a new plant was born and reached up for sunlight.

As you may have guessed, along with the plants came the weeds. It was my job to get them out of there. I didn't mind the hoeing, but I wasn't too keen on getting down on my knees and shuffling my way through the dirt to pull weeds. I did it though. After all, I sure didn't want Aunt Lou out there doing it with that new baby's birth only about four weeks away.

Aunt Lou loved her garden, and it was hard for her not to be out there picking weeds herself, but the doc had told her she would be wiser to let me do the pulling for this year. Reluctantly she agreed.

We were all counting the days till that baby joined us. The new crib Grandpa had fashioned was already in a corner of the little room that Aunt Lou called the nursery, the woven basket for the baby laundry beside it. Aunt Lou had made new ruffly white curtains and hung them at the window and framed a few pictures of somebody else's chubby babies to hang on the wall. Uncle Nat had bought a used rocking chair, revarnished it, and it sat there all ready for use with a knitted baby afghan tossed over one arm. The little chest was filled with baby clothes that Aunt Lou had sewed on her old machine, and on the crib, looking as good as any woman could have done by my way of thinking, was the baby quilt that Gramps had sweated over.

I stopped at the door and looked in on that little room 'most every time I walked by. We spent our time around the kitchen table discussing names and stating why we thought the baby would be a girl or a boy. It was fun planning together for the baby like that, and I think each one of us grew to love one another even more than we had before.

I was out there weeding in the garden late one afternoon when I got an awful urge for a cold drink of water. The afternoon sun could really beat down hot and made my throat dry and my skin prickly awfully quick. I stood up and stretched a bit and eyed the row ahead of me. I would easily finish it by suppertime.

When I got to the kitchen the potato pot was still sitting on the table with a half-peeled potato laying beside it. That was strange. Aunt Lou always had the potatoes cooking at this hour.

I listened, wondering if Aunt Lou had been called away for some reason. Then I heard a strange stirring from the bedroom, followed by a groan and my whole body went weak with the sound of it.

Aunt Lou lay on her bed, her face covered with her hands and a strange agony showing in the rigid way she was holding herself. Before I could even speak, another groan had escaped her and I ran to her side.

I was afraid to even touch her, so I just stood there, shaking, wondering what I should do and how soon Uncle Nat would be home.

Then she relaxed somewhat and took great gulping breaths of air. Her hands slipped down to rest on her full abdomen and I saw that her eyes were teary and pained looking.

"Aunt Lou?" I whispered.

She turned her head toward me and tried a weak smile.

"Oh—oh—Josh. Sorry, I—I'm not feeling so good."

"Should I find Uncle Nat?" I asked, wondering if I dared to leave her.

She nodded. Then she put out a hand to stop my dash.

"Get Doc first," she managed before another moan took hold of her.

I ran like I'd never run before, praying all the time I was running. *What if Doc isn't home, Lord?* I prayed. *What ever will I do?* Aunt Lou needed him, and she needed him *now.*

Doc was home. He was busy stitching up a cut on little Jeremy Sweeden's hand when I burst into his office room, calling out before I even reached him.

"Doc, come quick! Aunt Lou is awful sick."

Doc looked up from his stitching, his eyes showing immediate concern. But he didn't jump up and grab his black bag like I thought he should. Instead he said, "What is it, Joshua?"

"Aunt Lou," I said again, puffing out each word. "She's awful sick. She needs ya. Right now!"

"I'll come," he answered and turned back to his stitching.

"Right now!" I repeated almost shouting. I wanted to grab him by the arm and drag him to Aunt Lou's bedside.

"Yes, Josh. I'll be right there. Soon's I finish his hand."

It made me mad. I reckoned the hand wouldn't fall off or nothing if he left it, but who knew what might happen to Aunt Lou?

"You go on home and make sure there's a fire going and a kettle of water on," Doc told me. "I'll be right behind you."

I ran back to Aunt Lou, glad to have something to do. She was still groaning and tossing when I entered the house, and I nearly went wild with panic.

I guess it wasn't long till Doc joined us, but it sure did seem like forever. He didn't even stop in the kitchen to check on the fire or the water or nothing but went right on into Aunt Lou's bedroom and shut her door. I could hear the two of them talking in between Aunt Lou's groans. I checked the fire again to be sure it had lots of wood and then left again on the run. I had to find Uncle Nat, and I had no idea where he might be calling.

I ran all over the little town. I did find a few folks who said they had seen Uncle Nat earlier that day, but no one who knew where he was presently. At last, all tired out and panting, I turned for home. That was when I found Uncle Nat—at least signs of him. Poor old Dobbin stood at the hitching rail looking tired and hungry. Uncle Nat had deserted him and I was sure he was now in with Aunt Lou.

I took care of Dobbin, glad to be busy. I was very relieved that Doc and Uncle Nat were both with Aunt Lou.

After giving Dobbin his oats and brushing him down, I went to do my other chores. The woodbox still needed wood and the kitchen needed water even if Aunt Lou was sick. I left the unfinished row in the garden. I had no heart for it. The weeding could wait.

When I couldn't think of any more chores that needed doing, I returned to the kitchen. I wished there was some way I could just stay outside, but it was dark now and there was no reason for me to not go in. I hated the sounds of Aunt Lou's moaning. It made me hurt all over just to hear her.

I rumbled around in the kitchen peeling the rest of the potatoes and getting them on to cook. The smell of a roast baking was already coming from the oven. I didn't know what else she had planned to have for supper, so I went down to the cellar and took a jar of her canned beans from the shelf.

When I got back to the kitchen, Doc was sitting there on a chair at the table.

"Know how to make coffee?" he asked me, and I nodded that I did.

"Put on a pot, would you, Josh?" he asked me. "We could be in for a long wait until that baby decides to join us."

I stopped in my tracks, nearly dropping the jar of beans.

"Baby?" I said. "It's not time yet for the baby. It's not to be born until July."

"That's what we thought, but the baby has other ideas," said Doc knowingly.

"But it's too early," I continued to argue.

Doc sighed and drummed his fingers on the oil-clothed table. He raised his eyes to me and there was both sadness and hope there. Still he said nothing.

"Will she be okay?" I asked shakily. I was one who had voted for a baby girl. I wanted her to be just like her mother— so I would have a tiny Auntie Lou whom I could love and care for, just like Aunt Lou had cared for me when I was a baby.

"Can't say," said Doc quietly, and the whole inside of me trembled.

"Can't you stop it?"

Doc just shook his head; then he sighed a deep, sorrowful sigh.

"I've done all I can, Josh, but it's no use. This baby's going to come now."

I wanted to scream at him. To tell him he wasn't much of a doctor if he couldn't stop a tiny baby from coming before it should, but the words didn't come. Everything inside of me seemed to sort of freeze up.

Doc must have known how I felt. He cleared his throat and began to speak.

"We might have missed on the time, Josh. It happens. Remember, your aunt Lou was sick about then. But even if we didn't, and the baby is rushing things a bit, well, it still might be okay. Lots of babies have made it just fine even as early as your aunt Lou's will be. We just have to do everything we can—be ready to give him the best of care, and leave the rest to the Maker."

I somehow managed to put on the coffee Doc had asked for. I don't know how it tasted but Doc drank it anyway. He had probably tasted some pretty bad coffee in his day.

We had our supper. No one felt much like eating. Doc fixed a plate of food and took it to the bedroom for Uncle Nat, but it came back nearly as full as it had left the kitchen.

Along about eleven o'clock there was a knock on our door. It was unusual for someone to be calling at that time of night, and I didn't know just what to expect. It was Tom Harris. I knew he had been running pretty hard, in spite of the darkness. His eyes were sorta wild and he had a hard time talking because of his panting.

"Is Pastor Crawford here?" he asked me. I nodded my head that he was.

"We need him, right away," puffed Tom. "Old Sam is dyin'."

"What?" I couldn't help my question.

"Old Sam," went on Tom between gasps of air. "He's dyin'. He wants to talk to the parson."

"He can't come now," I told him frankly. "Aunt Lou is havin' her baby."

"But he's gotta! Old Sam won't last long. He said he has to see the parson."

I was about to shove Tom out the door when I heard Uncle Nat's voice behind me. "What is it, Tom?"

Tom told his story again and I watched Uncle Nat's face as he listened. I could see the agony deeply etched there.

"I'm sorry, Tom," Uncle Nat was saying, shaking his head. "I'm sorry, but I can't leave just now. Lou needs me here, I—I—I'm sorry."

Tom stood looking bewildered. He didn't leave like I figured he should have.

"He said not to come back without ya," he insisted.

"Where is he?"

"At the livery stable."

"You can't get him here?"

"He won't let us touch him. Says he'll die for sure iffen we try to move him."

"I'm sorry," said Uncle Nat in a tired, hurting voice.

Tom left then, slowly, sadly.

It wasn't long afterward that Uncle Nat came from Aunt Lou's room with his hat in one hand and his black Book in the other. I knew he was going to see old drunken Sam, our useless town bum.

"I'll take Dobbin," Uncle Nat said to himself as much as to me. "I'll be right back as soon as I can."

I guess I nodded or maybe even made some reply, I don't know, but deep inside me there was a feeling that this was wrong—all wrong.

Chapter 21

The Baby

Doc stayed in the room with Aunt Lou, and I paced back and forth in the kitchen. I guess I prayed. I don't really remember. I do know that I was hoping Uncle Nat would get back quickly.

I was annoyed with Old Sam. After all, Uncle Nat had talked with him many times about making things right with his Maker, and he never would pay him any heed, and here he was now, sick and dying and deciding that it was time he clean up his life.

Now, I didn't blame Sam none for not wanting to face God in his present state, but it did seem to me he could have picked a better time to start getting sorry for all his sins.

I guess I was a little annoyed with Uncle Nat, too, but I had the sense to know he had really been caught in a fix. I knew he really wanted to be here with Aunt Lou, and I sure knew that was right where Aunt Lou wanted him. I had heard little comments many times between them about how the two of them planned to share together in the birth of their baby. And now Aunt Lou was facing it alone.

The minutes kept ticking by. It was taking the old kitchen clock an unusually long time to move forward. I even thought about pouring myself a cup of coffee to give myself something to do, but I changed my mind. I never had cared for the stuff and often wondered how older folk managed to drink it.

It was right around midnight when I noticed there seemed to be more activity in the bedroom. I could hear Doc's voice talking to Aunt Lou. I couldn't tell if he was comforting her or instructing her. Soon I heard Aunt Lou give a little high-pitched cry, and then there was silence.

I strained to hear something, but there was nothing. The quiet was even worse than the moans had been. I walked slowly toward the closed bedroom door. I was almost to it when I heard Doc's voice again. I couldn't hear the words, but I could hear the tone and it made the fear run thick all through me.

Then there was a cry from Aunt Lou. It sounded like she said, "Oh, no! Please, dear God, no!" and then she started to sob. I could hear the loud crying right through the bedroom door and I wanted to fling it open and rush in to her. I didn't. I just stood there rooted to the spot, shaking and sweating and willing Uncle Nat to get back in a hurry.

He didn't. It was almost one-thirty and he still hadn't come. Doc had spent most of that time with Aunt Lou. She was quiet now and when Doc came back out to the kitchen, he looked old and tired.

"She's sleeping now," he said.

He knew very well that I wanted to know more than that. I couldn't ask. As much as I wanted to I couldn't ask.

"The baby didn't make it, Josh," said Doc, and that's all he said.

A thousand questions hammered at my brain, but I didn't ask a one of them. I couldn't. No words would come. I wanted to cry, but tears wouldn't come either.

"You should go to bed, Josh," said the doctor and he poured himself another cup of the strong black coffee with a rather shaky hand.

I didn't think I could sleep but I decided to go to bed anyway. I had to get out of that kitchen, to get off by myself somewhere. I turned to leave. Doc was stirring around in his black bag. He came up with a little bottle. He unscrewed the lid and a small white tablet fell into his hand.

"Take this, Josh," he said. "You'll sleep better."

Like a sleepwalker, I woodenly moved to do the doctor's bidding without giving it conscious thought. I put the pill in my mouth and lifted the dipper with water to my lips to wash it down, then headed for my bedroom.

Why isn't Uncle Nat back. Where is he anyway? If Old Sam is dying, he should have done it by now. My thoughts churned through my brain. I felt angry at both of them. Aunt Lou needed Uncle Nat. Or at least she *had* needed him. It was too late now. The baby was already dead. Aunt Lou had faced all the pain of it alone. She was sleeping now. *Most likely won't even hear Uncle Nat come in. What is keeping him anyway?* I raged.

Just as I reached the door I heard Doc's voice. He had lowered himself into one of the kitchen chairs and was sipping at the hot coffee, but he was talking to me.

"It was a girl, Josh. A baby girl."

I almost ran then, choking on the sobs that shook my whole body. I didn't even wait to undress, I just threw myself on my bed and let the sobs shake me. I cried for myself, for the loss I felt in not being able to love and care for that little baby. I cried for Aunt Lou in her pain of losing a child. I cried for the little baby, the tiny girl who would never know sunshine or flowers or the love of her family. And after I was all cried out, the bitterness began to seep into every part of me.

I was angry. Deeply angry. *God could have stopped all this.* At least if He was going to take Aunt Lou's baby, He could have left Uncle Nat with her to share her sorrow. But, no, Uncle Nat was gone. Out caring for some old drunk who had never listened to Him in all the months he should have been listening. So Aunt Lou had been all alone. Why? Didn't God care? Didn't He look after those who followed Him? After all, Aunt Lou and Uncle Nat were serving Him—were working in His church.

One thing I knew for sure, I would never be a minister. Not for anything. If a man couldn't even count on God to be with him and look after him, then what was the point of spending your life serving Him?

Maybe Mr. Foggelson was right. Maybe the Bible was a

book of myths. Maybe the whole thing didn't make any sense. *How do I know?* was my last hopeless thought. In a state of confusion and rejection, the small white tablet claimed me for sleep.

When I awoke the next morning, I was still in turmoil. I was still angry, too. I was not undressed, but someone had thrown a blanket over me some time during the night.

There were voices coming from the kitchen, and I forced myself to get off my bed. I wasn't too anxious to leave my room, but I couldn't just stay where I was. Reluctantly, I pushed open my door and stepped from the bedroom. I knew the voices then. I could hear Grandpa, then Gramps, and they were talking in soft tones to Uncle Nat.

When I finally forced myself to enter the kitchen, I saw that Uncle Charlie was there, too. There were coffee cups sitting on the table, but at present no one was drinking coffee.

A hush fell on the room when I entered, and I was embarrassed. I knew I looked a mess. My clothes were crumpled, my hair standing on end, and my face swollen from crying myself to sleep.

"Mornin', Boy," said Grandpa and he reached out an arm and pulled me to himself. I almost started crying again. Grandpa just held me close, like the holding would somehow lessen our pain.

Uncle Nat was there. I don't know when he returned. I didn't even care to ask him. Whenever it was, it was too late, by my way of thinking.

"You'll be happy to hear that Sam asked God to forgive him last night," said Uncle Nat, and I knew he considered that very good news.

I looked at the faces around the table and I could see that all of them shared Uncle Nat's feeling.

I nodded. So Old Sam had made his peace with God before he died. I knew that was good, but I just couldn't get too excited about it.

"Doc is carin' for him now. He's much better this mornin'."

"He didn't die?" I sputtered in bewilderment.

A gentle chuckle rustled from man to man around the table.

"No, he didn't die," said Uncle Nat. "He had himself a good scare though."

So he didn't die! He had called Uncle Nat away from Aunt Lou and then not even had the common decency to die. And as soon as he was back on his feet and able to stumble around the town, he'd be right back to his sinful ways too, I'd wager. It made me even angrier. I turned from the men at the table.

"I gotta get ready for school," I muttered.

Grandpa cleared his throat.

"Boy," he said, "iffen you're not up to it, you don't need to be goin' to school today."

I didn't want to go, but I didn't know what to do if I hung around at home either. Seemed to me there wasn't much for choices. Then I thought of Aunt Lou's garden. It still had some weeding to do. I mumbled a thanks to Grandpa and went to wash for breakfast.

It was a long, bitter day for me. The work in the garden helped, but all the time I weeded I could hear the saw and hammer, and I knew what was going on in Uncle Nat's shed. All four of the men were in there and they were working on a tiny coffin.

Every few minutes Uncle Nat would break from the others and go into the house to see how Aunt Lou was faring. If she was awake he would stay with her, but if she was sleeping he would come back out and help the men some more.

Doc called twice. Once in midmorning and once in the afternoon. He talked quietly to Uncle Nat, and I heard him say something about Aunt Lou being "as good as could be expected," and then he said that she was "accepting it well."

I finished the weeding and looked for other things to do. I cared for Dobbin and cut lots of firewood. Then I hauled water until I had all the buckets full.

The long day began to draw to a close. The menfolk took turns peeking in on Aunt Lou. I knew she welcomed the support of her family, but I just wasn't ready to see her yet.

The three men left for the farm, chores needing to be done.

They said that they'd be back again in the morning.

Uncle Nat spent most of the evening with Aunt Lou and that left me pretty much on my own. About the only thing I had to do was to answer the door. Already word had gotten around about Aunt Lou losing her baby, and pies and cakes and casseroles began to arrive at the house along with the condolences of the people of the parish. Even some of those who didn't go to church stopped by with a batch of cookies or a chicken pie and expressed their sorrow.

I was glad when I could finally shut the door, extinguish the light against more callers and go to my room. I was exhausted. I hadn't had much sleep the night before, and it had been a long and difficult day.

I must have gone to sleep fairly quickly. At least I don't recall laying and thinking none. I didn't want to think. And I sure didn't want to pray. I couldn't see much reason to keep on trying to be friends with a God who wouldn't care for His own.

Chapter 22

Adjustments

Somehow we got through the next few days. People came and went. The menfolk lined the small coffin with a soft blanket, and a service was held in the church with family members, parishioners, and many neighbors and town people. I'm sure it must have been especially hard for Uncle Nat, conducting the funeral for his own firstborn.

Aunt Lou was unable to attend the service, so Grandpa stayed home with her. I don't know what words he could say for comfort, but then maybe she didn't want words. When I walked by the door and glanced in, Grandpa was just sitting there by the bed, holding tight to Aunt Lou's hand.

I went back to school. The girls talked in hushed whispers as I walked by, and it angered me rather than bringing any solace. I wondered just what they knew about grief, and if they had ever lost someone that they had looked forward to seeing for so many months.

At home, the door to the little room known as the nursery was closed. I hurried every time I needed to pass it. Aunt Lou didn't. I saw her almost stop many times, as though to listen for the crying of a baby or the even breathing of a sleeping child. I wondered if she ever slipped in there when she was all alone and handled the tiny garments or straightened the quilt on the baby bed.

School was soon out for the summer and I was glad. A

change of routine sounded good to me.

Under usual circumstances I would have gone right out to the farm. But Aunt Lou was just beginning to get back on her feet again, and Grandpa felt I should stay around for a few more days to help her.

I didn't mind helping Aunt Lou, but I sure missed the farm. The open fields with wild strawberry patches, the crik with its fish holes, the clear, clean sky—all seemed to call to me. I needed to get away from town, I needed to get away from the little parsonage, I needed to get away from people. I would even have gotten away from myself if I could have thought of any way to do so.

There was no use fretting about it, so I just settled in and tried to make myself as useful to Aunt Lou as I could. She was getting stronger. She was even up and about in her kitchen. We still wouldn't let her out in her garden though, so I kept the weeds out the best that I could.

One day I went to the grocery store for Aunt Lou and nearly ran into Camellia on my way out. I could feel the red creeping slowly into my face and couldn't think of one thing to say to her, but she seemed composed enough. In fact, she even stopped and gave me one of her special smiles.

"Hello, Joshua," she said kindly. "How is your Aunt Lou?"

She sounded like she really cared, so I nervously shifted my package to my other hand and stopped to answer.

"She's getting lots better, thank you. She is even up now."

"Good," she said and then gave me another nice smile.

I looked around. I guess I expected Jack Berry to be lurking somewhere close at hand.

I was about to turn and go on my way when Camellia stopped me again.

"Would you care for some ice cream, Joshua?" she asked. Coming from anyone other than Camellia I would have considered that a pretty dumb question. Of course I liked ice cream.

"Papa gave me some money for a treat," Camellia went on, "and I do hate to eat all alone."

"Sure," I said, shuffling a bit awkwardly. "I'll have some with you."

I stopped thinking about Jack Berry. He really wasn't worth worrying about anyway.

We walked together to the sweet shop, and I held the door for Camellia. We settled ourselves at the counter on one of the high stools and gave our order. Vanilla for Camellia, chocolate for me.

Of course I had no intention of letting Camellia pay, and I was thankful that before leaving the house I'd had the good foresight to drop some coins into my levis.

"I suppose you've heard I am no longer seeing Jack," Camellia said casually. My head jerked up. She was looking down demurely and her lashes laid dark and soft upon her cheeks. I had almost forgotten just how pretty Camellia was.

I shook my head, that no, I hadn't heard that.

"Well, it's true," she continued. "He was just so dull. Papa never could endure him. Papa just detests a person with no wits, and Jack was certainly witless."

I couldn't have agreed more, but I didn't say so.

"Papa says he thinks that Jack has chalk dust where his brains should be," Camellia laughed. "He was just so boring. He couldn't reason a thing out for himself. Why, he couldn't even follow the thinking of a person who could reason. He never will make anything of himself."

She shrugged her shoulders carelessly. "So he has gone off to the big city. He said he's going to find a job and make all kinds of money and then I'll be sorry." She laughed again as though she found that hard to believe.

I sat there, not saying anything. I hated Jack Berry. Yet somehow it didn't seem right that Camellia, who had supposedly liked him, sat there and said such harsh things about him. But I pushed it all from my mind. What did I care about what had happened between Camellia and Jack, anyway? I looked at Camellia. She was as pretty as ever. Maybe even prettier.

She turned to me and said, "So what have you been doing, Joshua?"

I shifted nervously. "Oh, dunno. Nothin' much, I guess. Been helpin' Aunt Lou."

"I thought you might be at the farm," she commented.

"I will any day now. Grandpa thought I should stay a few more days till Aunt Lou gets a bit more of her strength back."

Our ice cream arrived—which I paid for—and we took a few bites before Camellia turned those blue eyes on me again.

"I've missed you, Joshua," she said softly and I nearly choked on my spoon. "Mama has missed you, too," she hurried on. "She has always said that you are the nicest and the bravest boy she knows."

I thought that that was awfully kind of her mother. I took another spoonful of ice cream so I wouldn't be expected to say anything.

"And Mama keeps telling Papa that being a preacher really isn't that bad," Camellia added.

"I've kinda changed my mind on that," I said rather slowly. "I don't think I want to be a preacher after all."

Camellia's face lit up.

"You don't?"

"Naw. I kinda got to thinkin' that I might like to be a lawyer. Or a university professor, maybe. I don't know for sure yet."

Camellia was giving me her biggest smile, her lashes fluttering as she did so. I knew she was pleased with my new direction in life.

I finished my ice cream and suddenly remembered why I had been sent up town.

"I've gotta get," I said. "Aunt Lou's waiting for this yeast."

I gathered my package and my cap and prepared to take my leave.

"Thank you, Joshua, for the ice cream," Camellia said, and then added so softly that only I could hear her words, "You're welcome to come over—any time."

I blushed and rushed from the sweet shop, sure that everyone must be staring after me. I glanced back at Camellia from the door. She was still sitting on the high stool, rhythmically swinging her legs back and forth. She gave me another of her smiles and then I was gone.

I was about to place the package on the kitchen table and run back outside but Aunt Lou stopped me.

"I have some fresh cookies, Josh. Would you like some?"

Now, normally I would not turn down such an offer. Aunt Lou prided herself on her cookies and I liked them, too, but I'd just had me a dish of ice cream. Still, I didn't want to refuse her, so I grinned, said, "Sure," and threw my cap in the corner.

Pixie always insisted on sharing my cookie time. I didn't object but held her close and fed her little broken-off nibbles now and then. These were the first cookies Aunt Lou had baked since—since she had been sick, and they sure did taste good all right.

"They're great," I enthused to Aunt Lou around the cookie that was in my mouth.

"I'm glad you like them," she answered and sat down in the chair next to me at the table. "Maybe now I'll be able to bake regularly again."

I sure was not blaming her for not keeping up with the baking, and I wanted to tell her so. But I didn't know quite how to say it, so I just reached for another cookie and fed Pixie another nibble before I popped the rest into my mouth.

"I haven't really talked to you about the baby, have I, Josh?" Aunt Lou said then, and I looked up, hoping that she wouldn't want to talk about her even now.

"You didn't even see her, did you?"

I shook my head. I'd had no desire to see Aunt Lou's baby.

"She was so tiny. So tiny. Why, she was almost lost in her nightie and blanket."

I could tell by Aunt Lou's voice that the memory of her little baby was both painful and pleasureful to her.

"We were wrong about her birthing time, Josh," Aunt Lou went on quickly. "She was full term."

My head came up then and I looked directly at Aunt Lou.

"Then why did she—?" I stopped short. I just couldn't say the word "die."

"Why did she die? Because she had some terrible deformities. You see, we didn't know it at the time, but Doc says now that I was already expecting the baby when I had the measles. You remember the measles, Josh? Well, measles can be bad for babies in the first few months—I mean, if the mother gets them. It can cause abnormalities—serious ones. We haven't talked much about it to folks because we don't want the Smiths to feel bad that I caught the measles while helping them. I didn't know about the baby then, or I would have stayed away."

I just sat there letting Pixie lick the crumbs of cookies from my fingers.

"Every day I thank God that He took our baby home to be with Him," Aunt Lou continued, and tears filled her eyes now. "Every day."

Aunt Lou is thankful that her baby died? I couldn't believe it.

"But—but I heard you," I stated rather sharply. "I heard you that night. You said, 'Please, God, no,' you said."

"Yes, I did," agreed Aunt Lou, and even though she was seated with me at the table, she somehow seemed far away. "My faith was small, Josh. I admit that to my shame. When I saw the baby and was afraid that she would live with her handicaps—her deformities—I said, 'Please, God, no'—not because I was afraid she might die, but because I was afraid she might live. Josh, I know that you won't understand this, and I'm ashamed to tell it, but I—I cried out to God to take her. I was wrong, Josh. I shouldn't have done that. I should have been willing to accept from God whatever was right for us and our baby."

The tears were running freely down Aunt Lou's face now. I'm not sure, but there might have been some on my cheeks as well.

"I did pray for the strength to accept God's will—later," went on Aunt Lou. "And I was finally able to honestly say, 'Thy will be done.' In just a few minutes after I uttered the prayer, God took her to be with Him."

I couldn't understand it. Not any of it.

"I am so thankful. So very thankful. Not for my sake, but for hers. Our baby is perfect now. She is no longer deformed. She will never be teased or tormented or made fun of. She will never suffer because of her handicaps or need to endure surgeries or painful hours. I do thank God for taking her."

I had eaten as many of Aunt Lou's fresh cookies as I could hold, so I just sat there ruffling the fur on the back of Pixie's neck.

"If she had lived, Josh, I would have found a way to thank God for that, too. I think that's some of the meaning in the word 'grace.' The Lord gives His grace to take what comes with thanks and faith. Do you understand that?"

I wasn't sure, so I didn't say anything.

"We called her Amanda, the name you had picked. Did you know?"

I did. I had heard.

"It hasn't been easy," Aunt Lou confided, "but I am glad to have a little jewel in heaven. Amanda. Amanda Joy. She did bring joy, even during the months we were planning and preparing for her. And it brings us joy to know she is safely in heaven, too."

Aunt Lou stood up and brushed away the last trace of tears with her apron.

"I know this has been hard for you, too, Josh," she said. "Why, you wanted that baby 'most as much as Nat and me. It's hard to give her up, I know that Josh, but we can be glad she is safe and loved and cared for by God himself." There was a brief pause, "And as soon as I am completely well and strong again, we are going to have another baby. We won't need to worry about the measles this time—that's over now. I know it seems like a long time to wait, but the months go quickly and before you know it, you'll have that little cousin you've been wanting."

Aunt Lou reached out and ruffled my hair, her smile back.

"We'll make it, Joshua," she said. "With God's help, we'll all make it."

I got up to go. I had wood to split and haul. I was glad, too, to be out of the kitchen.

I was really confused now. We had lost our baby—our Amanda Joy, but Aunt Lou said she thanked God every day for His mercy in taking her. How could I have known that God—in His will—had been answering Aunt Lou's prayer when He took Amanda Joy to heaven?

But I was still upset about Uncle Nat being away. If God wanted to care for Aunt Lou, He could have had Old Sam get sick at a different time—or the baby born earlier or later or something. There was no reason Aunt Lou should have been left to face the delivery of a severely deformed child, then the loss of it, all alone. Surely God could have worked things out much better than that.

I was really confused, but my anger still hadn't left me.

Chapter 23

Picking Up the Pieces

I visited Camellia once before I left town for the summer. I'm not sure how I felt about the visit. It was fun to sit and read books and chat about ideas again. It was great to be able to handle some of the interesting, colorful texts from Mr. Foggelson's library. It was good to see Mrs. Foggelson and get her pleasant smile of approval. I even enjoyed the tea and pastries—sort of—but all the time I was there I had this funny, nagging feeling deep down inside that I wasn't doing the right thing. I tried to ignore it, but it wouldn't go away.

Mr. Foggelson sort of hung around for a while talking about good books and showing me special pages that I should read. He even read a few paragraphs from a history book aloud to me to be sure I wouldn't miss them. Then he talked about the passages, asking me what I thought about this idea or that concept. I tried to answer the best I could, but some of them were things I had never heard of before.

I think Camellia and I were both glad when he finally left us on our own. Camellia told me over and over how "dull" she had found Jack Berry and how much she had missed my visits. I almost got to believing her. I did wonder why it had taken her so long to discover the fact of Jack's "dullness," but I didn't say so.

I still wasn't much taken with talk about Jack Berry. I

hadn't forgotten what he'd done to me. It was my right to feel pretty strongly about him, and I managed to keep quite a "hate" for him going.

In fact, whenever I wanted to spend some time feeling sorry for myself or getting a mad on about something, all I had to do was think of Jack Berry. I would let that little voice play over and over in my mind, *Jack Berry, Jack Berry,* and then I would think of the fist coming at me in the dark and the taste of blood and the sting of knuckle cuts and I would lather up real bitter feelings. Actually, I kind of enjoyed it. I must have—I did it often enough. It was the first time in my life that I had a really good excuse to get mad at the world.

Oh, I had been mad or upset about things in the past to be sure, but always I listened to this little voice saying, *Josh, this isn't right. You're not as bad off as you pretend to be.* But when it came to Jack Berry nearly killing me, I felt I had real good reason to nurse my anger.

Well, I only got that one chance to go over to Camellia's house and then Aunt Lou announced that she was feeling well enough that I should go on out to the farm like I usually did. She knew how much I missed it. Grandpa promised her that we'd slip into town every few days and see that she wasn't wanting for anything. Uncle Nat said that he'd see to it that she didn't do any water hauling or hoeing in her garden for a while yet, and I set off for the farm, anxious to get back to the familiar surroundings of green fields and wooded pastures.

Pixie was almost as glad to be back as I was. She spent the first ten minutes running round and round in circles and the next ten minutes checking out everything around to make sure it was just the same as when we had left it.

We all laughed at her, but I knew just how she felt. I was a little anxious to do some checking on my own, as well.

The place where I was heading was the crik, but I didn't want to appear too eager—just up and run for it the minute I got in the yard. But my family knew me well. I had just put my things in my room and returned to the kitchen when Grandpa turned to me.

"You suppose you might be able to catch us a fish or two for our supper, Boy?" he asked. I grinned and nodded.

"Hear they've been biting pretty good," added Uncle Charlie.

"What about my chores?" I asked.

"Reckon we can handle things for 'nother day," Grandpa assured me. "Catchin' us our supper will be your job for today."

"If you get some big ones," said Gramps with a wink, "then I'll go with you tomorrow."

So I was soon off to the crik.

My family must have known I needed this trip—and alone. I'd always enjoyed the company of Gramps. I would look forward to having him go with me on any of the days throughout the summer—except this one day. After so many things had happened, tearing me all up inside and confusing my thinking, I felt that my head was spinning. This day I needed to be alone.

The crik was about as pretty as I had ever seen it. The water was silvery ripples, almost as clear and clean as when it first splashed out of its hard rock bed at the spring up in the hills. The leaves were new green and they dipped and swayed in the afternoon breeze, flipping snatches of sunshine back and forth on the soft, still air. The birds were all a-twitter. They had finished their nest building and were busy now caring for young. Nearby a nest of baby robins called loudly to be fed, reminding me of the two babies at the last church picnic who had thumped on their high chairs with their metal spoons, making one awful commotion.

The thought of babies turned my thinking back to Aunt Lou and little Amanda. I still hadn't sorted through the hurt of it all. Aunt Lou was thankful that her little baby, her helpless little deformed baby, had been taken to heaven where she could be whole and without pain.

I knew Aunt Lou loved her baby so much she was willing to bear the pain of losing the little one if it meant something better for the baby. I knew that Aunt Lou hurt deeply. She said many times how much the prayers of the people kept her bearing that pain each day, and how she depended upon them. Well, I was glad that the people were praying for Aunt Lou. I wanted her to have all the help God could and would give her.

I still had some questions, though, and they wouldn't go away. Why did God let Aunt Lou get the measles in the first place? And why did He work it so Aunt Lou was without Uncle Nat when the baby was born and died? If God was really a God of love, why didn't He care for her better than that? I sure wouldn't treat someone I loved in such a fashion.

No, I just wasn't ready to forgive God. He could have worked it out much better. I didn't understand His ways at all. Did He *plan* for His people to hurt? I had heard preachers say that it was in such times that people learned to "trust" and to "grow." Well, there must be a better way than that. They were just trying to excuse God for His thoughtless actions, according to my way of thinking. I still had my mind made up. If God treated His good servants that way, then I sure wasn't going to be one of them.

I didn't know if He'd miss my service or not, but I guess I hoped that He would feel pretty bad about it. After all, that was about the only way I had of getting even.

I caught two nice-sized fish and felt pretty good about myself when I hurried home to show them off.

"Well, Boy," beamed Grandpa, "I guess you've earned your supper, right enough."

Uncle Charlie grinned too and took the fish to fillet them for supper.

"Do we have a date for tomorrow, Joshua?" asked Gramps. "I sure would like to catch one of those. I've been wanting to go fishing, but somehow it just isn't much fun for me to go on down to the creek without you. You willing to take an old man with you tomorrow? Is it a date?"

"Sure," I answered, nodding my head in agreement. "It's a date."

"Good!" said Gramps. "I'll get my hooks all cleaned up and ready."

Boy, did those two fish taste good. Even Pixie got in on it. I fed her tiny pieces of the fish after making good and sure there weren't any bones in them. She licked her little chops and begged for more. I let her lick at my sticky fingers instead.

We all went to bed early. I felt tired, though I couldn't understand why. I had worked lots harder on many days and not felt so all done in. *It's the excitement of coming home again,* I decided. I cuddled Pixie close on one arm and settled down to sleep. By now it didn't even bother me much that I hadn't taken time to say my prayers.

Willie rode his old horse Nell over for a visit one day. She was fat and lazy and a little clumsy, but Willie wouldn't have stood for anyone saying anything mean or teasing about her. He had ridden her since he had been just a kid in first grade, and he loved her just as much now as he had when she'd been a spirited young mare with her head held high and a prance to her step. I knew better than to make any cracks about old Nell.

We spent our time rubbing down the old horse and talking some boy talk about things we wanted to do with our summer. Already we were talking camping trip again. The further behind us our trip up the crik got, the better our memories of it. We were ready to go again the first chance we got. This time, though, we wouldn't try to shortcut through the Turleys' pasture.

"You know," remarked Willie, "I sure understand Avery lots better since that trip. He's a good kid, too. We spend lots of time together now. Was a time when I couldn't really understand what you saw in the fella. Used to make me kinda sore that you thought him your best friend 'stead of me. Now that I know him, I really like him."

I was a little surprised at Willie's words—not about his liking Avery now that he knew him better, but about him feeling kinda jealous because I had liked Avery a lot.

"His ma is feelin' lots better now," Willie went on. "An' I think Avery feels better about things, too. You know, Josh, he's grown a lot closer to God now that he isn't so scared an' he feels more sure of himself an' all. I think God really worked out that trip so's I could get to know Avery better and he'd have one more good friend."

Willie stopped and thought for a few minutes in silence. I guess I was doing some thinking, too. I had a feeling that Willie might be making a much better friend for Avery than I had ever been. Willie was helping him to understand God better. I had left Avery to do that sorting out all on his own.

"I'm not sure how it works," Willie suddenly said. "Do you get closer to God when you are not so scared about other things, or are you not so scared about other things because you are closer to God? What do you think?"

I looked at Willie's serious face, then shrugged my shoulders carelessly. How should I know which came first—if either?

I showed Willie all of Pixie's tricks, and then he wanted to see if she'd do them all for him. When she did some of them, he was real pleased with himself. He'd always wanted a dog of his own, he said.

We sat under the big poplar tree in the yard and ate cookies and drank some of Uncle Charlie's fresh lemonade until our sides ached. Then we decided to go down to the pond and try skipping rocks.

"Did ya hear that the School Board is lookin' for another teacher?" Willie asked off-handedly, slicing his rock against the surface of the pond.

I hadn't heard and my thoughts immediately went to Camellia rather than to her father.

"Why?" I asked Willie.

"They didn't like all the stuff he was teachin'. Like evolution an' everything."

I could believe that. I didn't think Grandpa would have been too happy either if he'd known what was being taught.

"That's why he got kicked out of his last school, ya know," went on Willie.

"Yeah," I replied as matter-of-factly as I could. "I heard." I didn't explain.

"When are they leavin'?" I asked next.

"He's still tryin' to convince the Board to let him stay," Willie answered. "Don't think there is much chance, though. Some of the members are really upset about it. They say it wouldn't have been so bad if Foggelson had taught it as theory, but he's been teachin' it as unquestioned fact—like it was the only way it could have happened. That's what they don't like."

"What do you think?" I asked.

"I don't think he should teach it as fact either. It mixes up some of the younger kids an'—"

"I don't mean that," I cut in.

"What do ya mean?"

"I mean, do you think it coulda happened that way? Like evolution?"

"Things just happenin' instead of God makin' them?"

"Yeah. Do you think it coulda?"

"Isn't what the Bible says. Sounds crazy to me. Actually, it's a lot harder to believe in evolution than in a Creator. What do you think?"

"Yeah," I agreed a little slowly. "It does sound rather crazy."

"You hear about Old Sam?" Willie said next.

"What?"

"He asked to be church custodian—without gettin' paid— just as a thank you to God for cleanin' his life up while there was still time. He's over there cleanin' an' polishin' every minute he gets. He's doin' a good job at the livery stable, too. They gave him a raise already."

"A raise?"

"Yeah—a little bit more money. They wanted to see first if he'd really be dependable—or iffen he'd just go off drinkin' again when he got his first wages. He didn't. An' Mrs. Larkin says he's a good boarder. Keeps himself an' his room nice and tidy an' comes to meals on time. He even helps some around the place."

I stopped throwing rocks and looked at Willie.

"Well, if that don't beat all," I declared, feeling some

grudging gratitude toward Old Sam. I knew it sure would help Uncle Nat out a powerful amount. He'd been doing the janitorial duties at the church along with all his other work.

We threw rocks until we spotted an old mother duck bringing her new hatching of ducklings to the pond for a swim, and then we flopped down on the warm, moist ground to watch them play around in the water.

I was still thinking of Camellia and questioning if she'd have to move away and wondering what she thought about it all when Willie cut into my thoughts again.

"Guess you must feel kinda special glad about Old Sam," he said.

"What do ya mean?" I asked.

"Well, about him making things right with God. None of us thought it could ever happen. We thought that Old Sam was too bad a sinner for God to even care about. Guess we thought he was goin' straight to hell. But there must have been some spark of conscience in him, for him to stop and help you when you fell in the dark and hurt your head like that, so you must feel good—"

I'd heard enough.

"I didn't fall!" I hissed, anger making my voice brittle.

Willie looked at me like I had lost my senses.

"I didn't fall," I said again. "It was that stinkin' Jack Berry—"

"What ya talkin' about?" exclaimed Willie, raising up on one arm so he could look me full in the face.

"Jack Berry," I repeated hotly. "He was there waitin' for me under that tree in the schoolyard. He was mad 'cause I was seein' Camellia and he liked her. He grabbed me and started punchin' me in the dark. I couldn't see who it was or anything. I tried to fight back—and I got in a few good punches, too—and then he hit me again and I slipped and ended up fallin' and hittin' my head on that rock, and that yellow coward ran off and left me there to freeze to death, for all he cared."

Willie sat right up and looked at me like I'd gone plumb crazy or something.

"Where'd you get that wild idea?" he asked.

"What d'ya mean?" I snapped back. "I was there, wasn't I?"

"Yeah, but you didn't say anything about any of that after you were hurt. You said you musta fallen. You said you couldn't remember."

"I couldn't. Not for a long, long time—an' then once after Jack started to see Camellia, he admitted it himself. Said he'd beat me up even worse the next time if I saw Camellia again."

Just thinking about it made my blood boil.

"Why didn't you say somethin'? I mean, after you remembered? Why didn't you tell us?"

"What good would that do?" I asked bitingly, and Willie nodded. He wasn't as riled up about the whole thing as I was, but still I could see it all troubled him. After all, he did consider me one of his best friends.

"That's about the most rotten thing I've ever heard," he stated at last. "How could Jack do such a thing?"

"That's good ol' Jack for ya," I said sarcastically.

"Did he ever say he was sorry?"

"Are you joshin'?" I scoffed. "He wasn't sorry, not ever. He would have done it all over again if he'd had the chance."

"That's rotten," said Willie. "Really rotten."

There was silence for a few minutes while Willie plucked at the grass and I hammered one little rock against another. I guess I was wishing I had Jack Berry's fingers between them.

"No wonder he didn't dare show up back at school," Willie remarked thoughtfully.

It was the first time I had thought about that, and I realized Willie was right. Jack likely did quit school because of the fight. Somehow the fact that he had lost something in the exchange brought me satisfaction.

"There's talk in town about Jack, too," Willie went on and his voice sounded a bit sad.

"What?" I asked, wondering if I was even interested.

Willie lowered himself back onto his elbow and started

pulling up little bits of grass that he threw to the side. He was stalling.

"What?" I asked again.

"You knew that Jack left town, went to the city."

I nodded. Camellia had told me that.

"I guess he and Camellia had a fight or somethin'. Least that's what the talk says. I don't know anything about it or what they was fightin' about," went on Willie.

"Maybe they didn't even fight," he surmised. "Maybe she just changed her mind, I don't know. Seems that Camellia, or her pa—I don't know which—thinks a fella should be smart an' make lots of money if he wants to call on her. Anyway, Jack left, an' he was plannin' to make himself rich real fast to impress Camellia or her pa. Well, I guess he tried—but not in the right way. Not many folks know much about it yet, but Jack landed himself in jail."

Willie looked so mournful when he said the words, like we should all be grieving over good ol' Jack or something. The whole thing hit me as funny—funny and terribly just. I threw back my head and laughed.

Willie looked up in surprise and then threw his next handful of grass at me.

"What's wrong with you, anyway?" he said hotly. "What's so funny about a fella bein' in jail."

"Nothin'," I answered, trying to control myself; "only it couldn't have happened to a nicer guy."

Willie gave me a stern look and pulled himself to his feet. He looked upset and Willie didn't get upset often.

Suddenly I was upset too. I sprang to my feet beside Willie.

"Oh, come on, Willie," I argued. "The guy jumped me in the dark and could've killed me. What do you expect me to say?" I changed my voice to a whining sing-song, "Poor, poor little Jackie. Someone has done him dirt."

Willie turned and looked at me, not pleased with my little charade.

"This is the real world, Willie," I continued, really in a lather; "the fella only got what's comin' to 'im."

Willie stood and looked at me for a long moment. "It doesn't hold up, Josh," he said, his voice even and controlled.

"Whatcha talkin' about?" I threw back at him, angry that he was now calm and I was still upset.

"You know what Scripture says about forgivin'."

"The jerk jumped me in the dark!" I insisted hotly. "What do you expect? That I'm just gonna say, 'I forgive you, Jackie. I know you didn't mean no harm'?"

" 'Course he meant you harm," agreed Willie. "Iffen what you say is right—an' I have no reason to doubt your word, Josh. 'Course he meant you harm. But is that what the Bible says? 'Forgive them only if they meant no harm'? No. It says 'forgive them.' Period. That's what Jesus did. Do you suppose Jack did you more harm than the mob did to Him?"

It was a silly question and we both knew it.

"He doesn't deserve forgiveness," I said, not ready to give in. "Anyone who would wait in the dark—and—"

Willie didn't even wait for me to finish.

"It's got nothin' to do with what he deserves. Can't you see that? You don't answer for Jack Berry; you answer for Josh Jones. The wrongs of Jack have nothin' to do with you. Aw, come on, Josh! What Jack did was pure rotten. Nobody's arguin' that Jack *deserves* your forgiveness, at least not in man's thinkin'. But God doesn't reason like that. Whether you forgive Jack or not really isn't goin' to hurt Jack Berry. It only hurts you, Josh. You happen to be my friend, an' I think that *you* deserve forgiveness."

"Me?" I said in shock. "What did I do?"

"Hate! Plan revenge! Hold bitterness! All those things are wrong and need forgiveness, too. God says He will only forgive us as we forgive others. I don't want you to be unforgiven, Josh." His voice broke.

Willie, my best friend, had tears in his eyes. He turned from me and kicked at a stone. I knew he was fighting to get back some control.

As I watched him, his words, and the truth of them, kept pounding through my brain. Wow! I hadn't thought of all that.

Willie was still swallowing hard. When he turned back to me, he was a bit pale and his voice trembled as he spoke.

"I gotta get home, Josh. I'll see ya Sunday," and Willie turned and left, traces of tears still in his eyes.

I watched him go. Inside I was all mixed up. I was still angry with Jack Berry. I still couldn't feel sorry that he had gone and got himself thrown into prison off in some big city somewhere.

Then I started to think about what it would be like to be in a big city all on your own and in some jail somewhere locked up, not knowing anyone and being shut away from the green grass and the blue sky. I guess I wouldn't like it much. *But he deserved it,* I kept telling myself. And then my mind flipped to some of the things that *I* deserved. I thought about my anger, hate, evil thoughts, selfishness—as bad as what Jack was in jail for.

The whole thing was so confusing. I didn't know what to think about anything anymore. I turned to the pond again and started throwing rocks, but my heart just wasn't in it. None of them "skipped." They just smashed into the blueness of the pond, then sunk to the bottom.

Chapter 24

A Fishing Trip

Gramps and I did go fishing a number of times. We usually took along a bucket with some lunch so we could sit and snack alongside the stream. In the clear, warm summer air it was cozy and relaxing and fun. Grandpa called it "lazy" weather. One sure didn't feel like doing much. You could use up a whole afternoon just laying on your back looking for funny shapes in the clouds or watching the new ducklings on the pond or something.

On one such afternoon as we headed for the crik again, Gramps looked up at the almost cloudless sky. "Ah-h, summer," he said. "Seems that God is always closest to earth in summer."

I wasn't sure if I shared Gramps sentiment, but I wasn't about to spoil our day by saying so.

We took off our shoes and socks, rolled up our pant legs and waded the crik to get to our favorite fishing hole. We spread our belongings out around us on the bank so we wouldn't have to get up for anything, then set about getting our lines in the crik water.

Before we even had time to drop a line in, a shadow swept slowly past in the water in front of us. We both nudged one another at the same time and leaned as far forward as we dared, to get a good look. It was all I could do to keep from jumping right in and trying to grab that big fish with my bare hands.

"Wow! Did you see him?" I whispered in excitement to Gramps. Almost at the same moment he said, "Did you see him? Biggest fish I ever saw! Oh, boy, Joshua, this is going to be fun!" and we both got serious about it, too excited to even think about munching on our sandwiches and brown sugar cookies.

Sorry to say, we never did see that big fish again, but we caught three others—two of them a nice size and the other a rather scrawny little thing. We kept it anyway. It would taste just as good as its bigger brothers and, anyway, its mouth was torn from the hook and we didn't want it to suffer.

Fishermen aren't much for visiting. I mean, you go fishing so you have you some thinking time. The notion that talk might scare the fish is just a ruse. What fishermen are really saying is, "Please don't interrupt the solitude. I'm communing with myself and nature out here."

When the sun swung to the west, we decided we should be getting on home, so we picked up our belongings and waded the crik again. Drying our feet on the grass, we sat down to slip back into our shoes and socks. We picked up all our gear and our empty lunch bucket and started down the trail to the farmyard. I was thinking of Camellia and how she might look at this quiet place when Gramps interrupted my thoughts.

"How's little Lou?"

I was surprised at his question. He had seen Lou just the day before, and I supposed he would have seen how she was most as good as anyone.

But Gramps went on. "You know Lou about as well as anyone does, Joshua. How do you think she is doing? I mean, way down deep inside?"

I thought I understood the question then, but I hesitated some before I answered.

"Good," I finally responded. "Quite good, I think."

"Thank God!" said Gramps and I knew he meant it from the bottom of his heart.

"Has she talked about the baby?"

"Yeah. Just a few days before I left to come home."

Gramps raised his white, bushy eyebrows. "What did she say?"

"Said she thanks God that He took the baby. Said that Amanda"—it was hard for me to call the baby girl by her name—"that Amanda is better in heaven. That she would have suffered a lot if she'd lived—and been made fun of, too."

Gramps shook his head slowly, then sighed deeply.

"She's right, Joshua. She's right."

Then Gramps said something I thought very strange.

"There are many things worse than death, Joshua. Many things. Oh, I know it is hard for those left behind. I still miss your great-grandmother terribly. Some days I think I just can't go on anymore without her, but God helps me and gives me strength and grace for each day." Gramps stopped to wipe his eyes, and then he went on, "That's not just a pretty phrase, you know, 'strength and grace for each day.' No, those are words with a lot of meaning. A lot of truth."

We walked on. I tried to tick the tree branches with the tip of my fishing pole without getting myself hung up on any of them.

Gramps went on. "When one is ready to meet his Maker, prepared and forgiven, then death is a welcome thing. I would not wish your great-grandmother back to endure the suffering of this world. Not to bring me comfort for even one day, one hour. I love her far too much for that."

It sounded strange to me, but I knew Gramps meant it.

"Lou is right about her little girl. She is much better off in heaven."

There was silence for many minutes. I thought Gramps had put aside his thinking on death, but he hadn't.

"When it comes time for me to go, I hope folks remember that I have finally had my hopes realized. That I have been taken home. I've felt lonesome for heaven for a long time now, Joshua. Ever since your great-grandmother left ahead of me, I guess. I can hardly wait to get there—can hardly *wait* to get there! Every day I have to ask the Lord for patience—for just a little bit longer. No, Joshua, I hope that no one, *no one* will ever grieve long for me."

My eyes were big and my heart thumping as Gramps said his feelings. I hoped with all my heart that God wasn't listening. He might decide to answer Gramps prayers right then and there. The very thought of it scared me half to death.

I started to try to voice a protest but Gramps kept right on talking. "Your great-grandmother's passing did bring about one good thing, Joshua." He paused and reached a soft, once work-roughened hand out to lay it on my arm. "If she hadn't left me, I might never have gotten to know you."

I swallowed hard. It was true. I blinked back tears when I thought of how I had fought against the idea of Gramps coming to join us—at first, that is. Now that he was here I wondered how we had ever gotten along without him.

"It's been good, my boy." Gramps had never called me that before. "I have loved our checkers, our chats, our choring," and he ruffled my hair, "and most of all our fishing."

I bit my trembling lip.

"You're a good boy, Joshua. I'm mighty proud of you."

There were so many things I wanted to say to Gramps. Like how I loved him, how much I enjoyed his companionship, his help, his just *being there*. Like how much more fun it was to come home to the farm knowing that he was there. But I didn't say any of them. I just didn't know how to put all those things into words.

"I'm getting to be an old man now. I've lived a full and good life. It won't be too much longer until the Lord calls me on home to join your great-grandmother. I won't need to be patient for much longer now." There was another pause. We were almost to the farm buildings now, and I guess Gramps figured that whatever else he had to say to me had to be said quickly.

"You are still very young. Your life stretches out before you. Don't waste it, Joshua. A life is far too precious to waste."

Mr. Foggelson had said that too, only a little differently.

He had said that a mind was too precious to waste—a good mind.

"The most wasteful, shameful thing that one can ever do is to fight against our Maker. He has only your good in mind, Joshua. His plan is the best possible plan for you to follow. Now, I don't know what that plan is. Only God knows. But whatever it is, Joshua, don't waste time and energy fighting against Him. Life is too short for that—even though right now it looks to you like you have almost forever. I'll be there waiting for you, Joshua, but when you come, I want you to come triumphant, because you have served God with all your energy, all your years, all your manhood—not head-hanging and ashamed. Do you understand me, son?"

I nodded. I thought I did.

"Let Him lead you, Joshua—every step of the way. Don't ever question Him and don't ever detour off His path. It's far too costly."

I nodded solemnly. I wondered if Gramps had been reading my mind. It made me feel a mite uncomfortable.

By then we were entering the path that led up to the house. I knew that Gramps had no idea of the turmoil that was going on inside me. I was glad. I wouldn't have wanted him to know. He would have been ashamed of me. Of the way I had been thinking and feeling.

I was glad we were home, that I had chores to do. I was anxious to slip away by myself so that my feelings wouldn't show. I was swallowing hard to keep the tears from coming. I knew Gramps hadn't said his words to upset me. He loved me and had no idea of the thoughts I had been burying deep inside. The thoughts of hate for Jack Berry. The doubts and frustrations about the Bible and evolution. The bitterness about little Amanda Joy. The feelings about God not caring for His people. I was glad Gramps couldn't see my heart. He would have been saddened by what he found there. I loved Gramps and would have died before I would have intentionally hurt him.

I tried to give Gramps a smile before we parted company but it was a bit shaky.

He patted my shoulder once more and gave me one of his big smiles that twitched his trim mustache and made his eyes twinkle. I loved Gramps. I hoped he would be with us for many years to come. I just couldn't imagine what life would be like without him.

Chapter 25

Lessons in Living

I did a lot of thinking during the next few days. The conversations I'd recently had with Willie and Gramps kept playing over and over in my head. My conscience told me that what they had said was true. I knew I had no rights that gave me the privilege of hanging on to anger and bitterness against Jack Berry. God had commanded us to forgive others, even when they had given us cause to hate instead.

I knew, too, that baby Amanda truly was better off in God's heaven. Grandpa had talked with me about some of the severe abnormalities of the baby. If she would have lived—and Doc could see no way that she could have possibly survived, but if by some miracle she had—she would have needed hospitalization and many operations to make it possible even to feed her. We would have loved her, we all knew that, but she would have suffered terribly, both physically and from mistreatment by others.

But I still blamed God. Not only for the fact that baby Amanda was born as she was, and then died so quickly, but because Aunt Lou had needed to face it all alone.

Old Sam hadn't gone back to his drinking like I was sure he would. He was still holding down his job and keeping himself and his rented room neat as could be. He was taking good care of the church as well, and sang, intelligibly now, as he worked.

I went to town at least twice a week, stopping in to see Aunt Lou and to help her with her garden. I split and carried the wood for her, too. Aunt Lou was getting stronger every day, and though she still grieved over her baby, the anguish was gone from her eyes. She could smile again and she could even laugh. I loved hearing her sing the old hymns softly to herself as she went about her daily tasks.

"Isn't it wonderful to watch Sam polish up the church?" she said to me one day as I sat at the kitchen table. She probably thought of that 'cause I was polishing up a new fishhook I was dying to try. "Whoever would have believed that God could change him so much." She went to stand at her kitchen windows, one hand holding back the lacy curtains so that she could watch Old Sam washing the church windowpanes. She laughed softly.

"That's silly, isn't it? Of course God can change a man. He changed me when I asked for His forgiveness. It just shows up in different ways, that's all."

She let the curtain slide back into place and returned to her bread-baking.

"When I think how Nat nearly didn't go that night, it scares me."

I looked up then. Aunt Lou noticed and continued.

"Oh, Nat wanted to go. He wanted to go very much, but he didn't want to leave me and Amanda." Aunt Lou was finally at the point where she could talk about Amanda, even call her by name, without weeping.

"He knew he should go and he longed to go, but he wouldn't leave me. It was awfully hard for Nat. I had to *insist* that he put his calling to the ministry before his family. God was asking him to go to Sam! There was no one else to go, and an hour, two hours, might be too late, forever. Doc was with me. I knew I'd be all right."

Aunt Lou gave the bread one more brisk roll, then plunked it back in the pan and gave it a firm pat. She recovered it with the clean, white kitchen towel and pushed it back out of her way.

I was still chewing over her words. *Aunt Lou* had insisted

that Uncle Nat go to Old Sam. I hadn't known that.

"How did Uncle Nat feel when he got back?" I asked, trying not to let Aunt Lou know that the question was loaded with all sorts of implications and accusations.

"Poor Nat," she said, her eyes clouded. "He felt just terrible. Not only was he grieved with losing our baby, but he was so sorry he hadn't been there with me."

I nodded. *He should have felt that way,* I reckoned. And God could have done something about the whole thing.

"I told Nat that it was okay. That I knew why he was gone. I prayed for him the whole time he was away that God would give him the right words, so Sam would understand how much God loved him in spite of his sin—that God was waiting to forgive him if he'd just ask.

"And—" Aunt Lou hesitated. "This is hard to put into words, Josh, but it was the strangest thing. I didn't miss Nat. I mean, I felt like I was there with him, sharing in his ministry to Sam, and I felt that he was here with me, sharing in the birth of our first baby. I think it was God—I mean, I think because God has made us one, and because it was a special time for both of us, that God sorta bonded us together in love even though we were apart."

Aunt Lou reached out a hand to my shoulder and smiled.

"I'm sure that none of this makes much sense to you, Josh. Maybe someday, when you grow older and fall in love and marry some sweet girl, you will know more what I am talking about."

"You're right," I nodded. "It don't make much sense. I thought you wanted Uncle Nat right there with you."

"Oh, I did," she quickly responded. "And if it would have been for any other reason that Nat wasn't there, I would have been really upset. I mean, if he'd been off fishing or just off with the menfolk chatting or something—but it was his duty, not his desire, that took him away from me, and I can understand and accept that."

"His duty?" I muttered.

"Yes, he had to go. Sam needed him."

"You needed him, too. He left you all alone—"

"No, not alone. Never in my life had God seemed so close. He was right there with me, wrapping me in His love, holding me tight when I needed comfort."

Aunt Lou stopped for a moment as though once again sensing the special feelings of those hours spent with God. Then she went on again. "No, Josh, it was Sam who needed Nat. He might have died without his sins forgiven and gone out into eternity without God."

"He didn't even die," I reminded her.

"How were we to know that? At least he was ready that night when he was afraid he might die, ready to call on God for forgiveness. If Nat had missed the opportunity, Sam might have thought that Nat really didn't care and he might never have become a believer."

"I dunno," I said carelessly, still polishing the new fishhook. "Seems like pretty bad timing to me."

Aunt Lou crossed back to the window and lifted the curtain again. She stood there watching Old Sam, her eyes brimming with tears. They spilled down her cheek and she didn't even bother to wipe them away.

"Seems like perfect timing to me," she said in almost a whisper. "At the same moment I was losing the child that I wanted and loved, God was reclaiming one of His children for His very own. He loves Sam as much—no, even more—than I love Amanda Joy. Every time I think of little Amanda, I am reminded of the night, the very hour, when Sam came back to the Father."

Aunt Lou just stood there, the tears still unchecked on her cheek. Then she let the curtain drop again and turned to me with a trembly smile.

"God received two children that night, Josh. One through death, one through rebirth. It's beautiful, isn't it?"

Summer slowly crept toward autumn. The School Board decided to let Mr. Foggelson have one more chance and school started as usual. I only missed the first week to help with the harvest. Then it rained so I hustled to town to try to catch up on my schoolwork.

I didn't admit it to anyone, but I was relieved that Camellia wouldn't need to move away. I went to see Camellia again on Thursday. I felt rather funny and uncomfortable about it, but because I enjoyed her company I went again the next day before I headed to the farm for the weekend. Mrs. Foggelson joined us for tea. I tried to relax and enjoy her tea and pastries, but I felt her sharp blue eyes upon me, as though they were trying to pierce through me to find some answers. Was I going to compromise like she had done? Would I let her down? Had Mr. Foggelson, with his sharp mind and his eloquent tongue, gotten through to me just as he had to her?

Later, Camellia and I tried to talk about books just like we had always done. It was hard for me. I had so many things churning around inside of me. On the one hand were all my doubts. On the other hand were the Bible truths I had learned from the time I was a child. I couldn't really swallow evolution and the supposed facts that it presented. It was like Willie said. It was just too unbelievable.

No, try as I might, I could not believe that things just happened. I did believe in God. *There has to be a God*, I concluded. I guess I had never really doubted that, not even for a minute. What really had been troubling me was how God related to folks as individuals.

Was it true what we had learned in church? Was it true that God knew the best for each life, that He cared for those who followed His way? I had thought He had let Aunt Lou down. But Aunt Lou said that He hadn't. She said that she had never felt God's love as strongly about her. That was rather peculiar. To be going through such pain and yet feeling God's love the most.

And then there was this thing about Jack Berry. I hadn't shaken Willie's words. He said that whether Jack deserved forgiveness or not, I did, and the only way I could find that forgiveness, for my hate and my bitterness and my desire to get even, was to ask God to forgive me.

Boy, it had me all mixed up.

I stole a glance at Camellia. I had never really faced it

before, but she was my other problem. I knew Camellia and her pa had their hearts set on a smart young man who could make lots of money and buy her lots of nice things. I knew Mr. Foggelson thought that a fella who believed the things that the Bible said couldn't be all that smart, and therefore he likely wouldn't make much money and so he'd never make his daughter happy.

I thought Camellia was pretty special. I knew that my faith in God and my choice of a friend weren't very compatible. Not that I was thinking on getting married or anything. I mean, I wasn't even sixteen yet—neither was Camellia, but well—she was really pretty and . . .

If I told Camellia that I believed what the Bible said was true, she'd tell me not to bother coming back, I was just sure of it.

Then another idea came to me. I'd pray. I'd pray that Camellia and her ma and pa would change their thinking. That they would start to go to church and believe the things the Bible taught. Then Camellia and I could still go on seeing each other.

Even as I got excited about the thought, I knew it was wrong. Sure, I should pray for Camellia. And for her folks, too. But not so I could go on seeing her. That was the wrong kind of an attitude. I should pray for her because I cared about her, and because I cared about her ma and her pa, too. They needed to turn to the Lord. They needed to recognize that things didn't just accidentally fall into being, that there is a Creator. Things didn't just evolve. And because God really was God, He had the right to ask His creation to walk in His ways.

Wasn't there some way I could hang on to God, my anger and Camellia, too? Did a person have to turn over *every-thing*—every part of life when he asked God to direct his ways? Wasn't there some way I could still choose some areas where I could still be in control?

And then I started thinking on Gramps' words. Gramps seemed pretty sure that wanting to take things in your own hands was fighting against God. And Gramps felt pretty strongly that doing so was not only stupid and wasteful, but sinful and disastrous.

The whole thing had my head spinning.

But I couldn't chat with Camellia about her pa's books and be working that all out, too, so I tried to push all the conflicting thoughts from my mind.

"Do you or don't you, Joshua?" Camellia was asking.

"Huh? I mean, pardon? I guess I was thinkin'—"

"About something else. I know. I just hope it wasn't another girl," teased Camellia.

" 'Course not," I said, blushing to the roots of my hair.

"I wanted to know if you'd like to come with us for a picnic on Sunday. We are going to the lake."

"Oh!" I answered. "Oh, no, I can't. It's church."

Camellia looked hurt.

"Can't you skip church for just one Sunday?" she pouted. "You go to your old church all the time. 'I can't come over on Wednesday, Camellia. I have to go to meeting. I can't see you on Sunday, I have to go to church,' " she mocked. "I'm beginning to think—"

"I'm sorry," I interrupted.

"Then you'll come?"

I looked at her steadily. I think I realized at that moment that Camellia would never understand me—not really.

"No," I said firmly. "No, I can't come. I'm going to church."

Her temper flared. "Well, if your old church is more important to you than I am, then you—"

"I'm sorry," I said rather sadly. "I'm sorry, but I guess it is."

I thought Camellia would strike out angrily. But she didn't. In fact, she changed her approach completely, even giving me a smile.

"I'm sorry, Joshua," she said almost sweetly. "Let's not fight. If it is that important to you, then, by all means, go ahead. I'll tell you all about the picnic when you come over next week."

I reached for my cap and fumbled it around and around in my hands. It seemed a long time until I was brave enough to say it, but I finally managed.

"I'm sorry, Camellia," I said in a low voice. "I—I won't be comin' next week."

"What do you mean?" Her voice sounded angry and almost frightened.

"I won't be comin' back. I shouldn't be here now. I—I can't agree with your pa's books about evolution an' all those other things. I can't agree that bein' smart is the greatest thing in the world either. I don't think that makin' lots of money is the only way to live. I—I think different from you. I—I believe that church is important. I believe that God is important. I know I haven't been livin' like it but—but—"

I fumbled with my cap some more.

"Right now I'm all mixed up. I've been tryin' to hang on to God and live for Josh Jones, too. It doesn't work so good." I looked down at my cap. It was a while before I could go on. "I've got a lot of things all mixed up. I need some thinkin' time," I finished lamely. Then I made myself move quickly to the door before I could change my mind or Camellia could protest. I was anxious to get back to the freedom of the farm and the busyness of the harvest fields and the familiar chores.

"Bye, Camellia," I stammered and I almost ran from the room, anxious to get away, somehow thinking I could escape also from all of the conflicting thoughts that were tearing away on the inside of me.

Chapter 26

The Beginning

I awakened earlier than usual the next morning—not by my choice. I had slept poorly the night before, still wrestling with some of my conflicts. I knew that my life really belonged to God. I knew that I would most likely be happier, be at peace inside, if I let go of all my self-will and let Him direct me. But for some strange reason I just didn't want to do that.

So I was still needing more sleep when a commotion in the big farmhouse awakened me. It took me a few minutes before I could get myself awake enough to sort out the noises. It was Grandpa.

"Charlie!" he called. "Charlie—get down here quick!"

I heard Uncle Charlie as he hit the wooden floor in his bedroom and hurried to the steps. It sounded, by the strange thumping noises, like he was trying to get into his trousers and run at the same time.

"What is it?" he called back to Grandpa from the head of the stairs.

"It's Pa," said Grandpa.

The words sent a chill all through me. "Pa" to Grandpa was "Gramps" to me, and I didn't like the way Grandpa had said the word—his voice tight with emotion.

I was out of bed in a flash, and I never even stopped to pull on my pants, just grabbed them and somehow worked them on as I ran.

Uncle Charlie and Grandpa were already in Gramps' room. I came running up behind them and tried to push my way between them. Grandpa put out a hand to stop me, but I put my weight against it and forced my way by.

"What's wrong?" I demanded. "What's wrong with Gramps? He sick or—?"

I stopped abruptly. Gramps lay still on his bed, his eyes closed, a faint hint of a smile on his relaxed face. There was no gentle lifting and falling of his chest with his breathing. All was quiet. Too quiet. Grandpa moved close behind me and placed a hand on my shoulder.

"Yer Gramps is gone, Boy," he said, and his voice trembled.

"No!" I shouted. "No!" and I brushed away Grandpa's restraining hand that was meant to comfort me and dashed from the room.

I don't know how I got to the fishing hole. I don't know how long I lay there on the cold damp grass. I only know that when I had finally cried myself all out, that's where I was.

I didn't even try to get up. The grass was dew-wet and the morning foggy and cold. Suddenly a shiver made me realize just how cold I was. Laying right beside me was my choring jacket and my flannel shirt. Someone had visited me—and I hadn't even noticed.

I crawled awkwardly into my clothes, shivering as I did so. My body was damp from the wet grass, and the flannel felt good on my back.

I tried hard to pull myself together, but it was tough.

I walked down to the crik and bent low to splash cold water on my puffy face. Just as I bent over the cool water, a dark shadow approached, then just as quickly disappeared beneath some low branches hanging from the willows at the crik's edge. It was that big northern again—the one Gramps and I had seen on our last fishing trip together.

The sight was too much for me. I lowered my body to the sandy bank and let my mind drift back. The sobs overtook me again. It had been fun to fish with Gramps. He was great company. I would miss him. Boy, would I miss him! He had talked to me man to man. Just like we were equals.

My mind filled with some of those things Gramps had shared. He had said that he was lonesome. That he wanted to go home to heaven. That it was hard for him to be patient, knowing that Great-grandma was waiting for him there and all.

He had said something else, too. He said, "I don't want anyone grieving long for me." Strange he should say that— just a few short days before he went home, too.

I sorted through my memories to try to remember all of Gramps' words. He had talked quite a lot about death that day. I hadn't paid much mind to some of what he had said at the time. I didn't like thinking about death.

But he had talked about more than death. He had talked about life, too. About how to live it. That I was to be sure to let God have complete control of every part of my life. That I was to be ready to die, whenever that time would come.

That meant I couldn't hang on to bitterness or anger, no matter how much I had a right to be mad. I guess I couldn't hang on to my future either and make my own plans about what I wanted to do. It meant that I couldn't blame God for things happening when they did or how they did—especially when it all turned out right and good anyway.

Either God was God—or He wasn't. There was no moving Him in and out of my life with the mood I happened to be in.

All sorts of things started to fall into place for me. I saw some things clearer than I ever had before. I think I saw Gramps—his life and what he had tried to teach me—more clearly, too. I understood what he was trying to say to me about him being there waiting for me, and how I was to join him "triumphant" because I had been obedient to God, and not with my head hanging in shame.

As I thought of all of these things, I just lay there on that cold ground sobbing my heart out. Only this time I wasn't grieving for Gramps. I was grieving for me. I sure had messed things up. I had filled myself so full of anger and bitterness and pain and doubts, and then I had turned right around and pointed my finger at God as though He was to blame for it all. I knew better. Deep down I knew better. How could a God who loved me enough to die for me turn around and be spiteful and mean?

I cried it all out to God, asking Him to forgive me and to take away all of the bad feelings I had inside. I told Him I was done making my own plans. I didn't know if He wanted me to be a preacher like Uncle Nat, but that didn't matter. What *did* matter was that I was *willing* to be one—if that's what God wanted me to be. If He wanted me to be a farmer, I'd be that. Or if He wanted me to be a lawyer, or a doctor, or even a teacher, I would try to be the best one I could possibly be.

And then I prayed—sincerely—for Camellia and her ma and pa. I prayed that God would help them to understand how much He loved them and how sad He was that they couldn't believe in Him. I prayed for Mrs. Foggelson in another way—that she might have the courage to come back to her faith.

I even prayed for Jack Berry. Not because I *should*, but because I really wanted to. All of a sudden, I felt so sorry for Jack. He had hated school, but his pa had insisted he be a doctor. He had even been gypped out of the camping trip, and he had wanted to go as much as any one of us. He had liked Camellia, but that hadn't worked for him either. He had wanted to do great things and prove himself important, and here he was, alone, in some musty jail somewhere, no one able to visit him or even caring much that he was there. I really felt sorry for Jack Berry.

I can at least write to him, I decided. Maybe if he knew I wasn't out to get him, we could be friends again. And maybe he'd believe me when I told him about God's love.

And then I prayed for my family. The sad news would need to be taken to Aunt Lou, and I knew how much she had loved Gramps. Uncle Nat would need to conduct the funeral service, and that would be awfully hard for him. He had loved Gramps, too.

And Uncle Charlie and my grandpa—they would hurt

something awful. We had all grown to need Gramps among us. He had been a strength, a source of laughter. We sure were going to miss him.

I got up and washed my face again. The shadow moved. I spoke out loud.

"It's all right. You're safe, ol' northern. I'm gonna leave you there. For Gramps. He shoulda caught you. You know how excited he woulda been to have landed you? He'd a shouted all the way back to the house."

I couldn't help but laugh just thinking about it. The laughter surprised me.

And then I turned my face heavenward and laughed again. How could one feel joy and sorrow at the same time? Yet I did. I felt good inside—clean and good. And yet I hurt. Oh, I hurt bad. I was smart enough to know I would hurt for a long time to come. I just couldn't think of life without Gramps. But I wouldn't grieve. For his sake, I wouldn't grieve because he had asked me not to, because he was now in heaven where he longed to be. I loved him so much that I'd let him go.

I turned my steps homeward. A feeling of peace stole over me. Maybe that was what Aunt Lou had tried to tell me about. God's love. God's love there to hold me when I needed His comfort so much.

I took a deep breath. It was strange. The whole thing was strange. I had nearly thrown away my faith when I had lost someone that I loved—and here, at the loss of someone else I loved, I had had it restored again.

" 'God works in mysterious ways,' " I repeated to myself. I had heard Uncle Nat say those words, but I'd never really understood them before.

And then I looked at the sky above me, a soft blue with puffy little clouds drifting carelessly toward the south. The trees along the path seemed to whisper little secrets as the wind gently rustled the leaves. Early fall flowers were blooming under the branches, spreading their fragrance to make the woods a sweetly scented place to be.

I looked back at the sky, much as Gramps had done such

a short time before, and repeated the words I had heard Gramps say on that day—for both of us, "Aw, summer. In summer it seems God is closer to earth than any other time of year."

I wouldn't argue with Gramps. God did seem close to the earth that summer as Gramps and I had shared our fishing trips and our chats. Summer would always be more special to me now, too.

But I had always been rather partial to the autumn. I looked about me. Already the leaves were subtly changing color, and just beyond the trees I could hear the neighbor men busily working in their wheat field. I loved autumn— and harvest.

My time of walking the path to the crik with Gramps was over. I would miss it. I would miss him! But somehow my life would go on. Gramps' life would go on, too. He was just living in a different home now, that was all. It was not the end. It was really a beginning. A new beginning for both of us.